Picture Perfect

ETERNAL REST
BED AND BREAKFAST

PARANORMAL COZY MYSTERIES

BETH DOLGNER

Picture Perfect
Eternal Rest Bed and Breakfast Book Three
© 2021 Beth Dolgner

All rights reserved. No portion of this book may be reproduced in any form without permission from the publisher, except as permitted by U.S. copyright law.

ISBN-13: 978-1-7365724-5-0

Picture Perfect is a work of fiction. Names, characters, places, and incidents either are the products of the author's imagination or are used fictitiously. Any resemblance to actual persons, living or dead, businesses, companies, events, or locales is entirely coincidental.

Published by Redglare Press
Cover by Dark Mojo Designs
Print Formatting by The Madd Formatter

BethDolgner.com

Emily stifled a yawn, then coughed as a wave of smoke rushed into her throat. "Is it really necessary to get inside the cabinets, too?" she croaked.

"Yes! You want to cleanse the entire house, and that includes inside the wardrobes and cabinets." Sage's voice was strained, like she was holding back a laugh. "You're only supposed to stick the sage into the cabinet, Em, not your head, too!"

Still coughing, Emily straightened up, a smoking bundle of dried sage in her hand. "Well, I wanted to make sure I got it all the way under the sink. That takes care of the kitchen, at least. Only one room left to go."

Emily moved across the hall into her bedroom, waving the sage slowly as she had been instructed to do. As her best friend and a psychic medium, Sage had been only too happy to teach Emily how to cleanse her house of negative energy. The fact that the necessary herb shared her name only made Sage that much more enthusiastic. Sage followed Emily into the room, and within ten minutes, the ritual was finished. They had started all the way up on the third floor, in the little gabled room that Emily used for storage, and worked their way down. Emily's friend Reed had done the opposite, starting all the way down in the storm cellar before heading to the old barn behind the house.

Before they had begun, Sage had put two small plates outside: one on the front porch and one on the back steps. Now, Emily took her sage bundle onto the front porch and placed it on the plate there, where it would eventually burn itself out. Sage put hers on the back steps.

The fresh air felt nice after the smokiness inside the house. Emily actually liked the smell of the burning sage, but the air inside Eternal Rest Bed and Breakfast was saturated with it. Absently, Emily reached over her shoulder and pulled the end of her low ponytail toward her face. She sniffed at the light-brown hair and wrinkled her nose. It smelled just as strong as the house. Emily let go of her ponytail, took a deep breath, and plunged back inside.

Reed was just coming in the back door, and he gave Emily a thumbs up as she waved him in the direction of the parlor.

"Time for tea, then!" she announced, passing Reed to go into the kitchen.

When Emily joined her friends in the parlor with a tray of sweet tea, she found Sage sitting on the sofa with a satisfied expression on her face. The ankh pendant around her neck gleamed against her gauzy lilac dress. She gratefully accepted a glass of tea from Emily, who settled into one of the red wingback chairs that flanked the sofa. Emily sighed happily as she turned her head to gaze through one of the floor-to-ceiling windows that provided a view of the front porch and the two-lane road that led into downtown Oak Hill. The sun had already set, and the twilight sky was a mellow gold, unmarred by a single cloud. "It's a good sign," she murmured.

"Agreed," Sage said. "This was a good idea, Emily. Even the ghosts feel happy about it."

"I'm glad they understand that we did this to clear out anything negative, and not to clear out them."

"Your ghosts were decent people in life," Reed said reassuringly. "I'm sure they know you'd never want to get rid of them."

Emily sighed again, but this time there was a worried sound to it. "I just hope it helps."

Sage leaned toward Emily. "Remember, we don't know what's preventing Scott's spirit from communicating with us," she said in a matronly tone, "but everything we do to make it easier for him will help. Still, I don't want you to expect some kind of miracle. Whatever is keeping your husband from coming back to Eternal Rest is also keeping him from coming to me for a little chat, which indicates he's barred from Oak Hill altogether."

Emily nodded as she chewed her lip thoughtfully. "You mentioned once before that it's almost like there's a spiritual barrier around Oak Hill. Scott was able to communicate with Reed's cousin in Alabama, but for some reason he can't make it to Georgia."

Reed chuckled darkly. "Let's hope the barrier doesn't cover the whole state. We can chip away at something the size of a town, but I don't know about all of Georgia. Of course, that's assuming it is some kind of barrier, and not a negative entity keeping Scott away."

"Either way," Sage broke in, "every little bit helps. Besides, considering some of the living people who have been under this roof recently, I think a cleansing was necessary."

"Agreed. Jaxon Knight-MacGinn was an angry, stuck-up jerk." Emily paused, suddenly feeling disrespectful of the dead. She added quickly, "May he rest in peace."

Sage rolled her eyes. "I meant the murderous guest you had staying here, as well as your murderous assistant."

Emily felt herself blush at the oversight. "Oh, well, sure.

Them, too." Emily leaned back and stared up at the ceiling. She was used to a fairly quiet life at Eternal Rest Bed and Breakfast. Yes, the house was usually buzzing with the activity of her guests, but it was a relaxed kind of energy. Most people who stayed there were good people enjoying a little getaway from their busy lives. If they chose to spend their vacation days staying at a haunted bed and breakfast, or even actively looking for the ghostly residents of the Victorian house, then that was their business. Actually, it was Emily's business, too—quite literally—and she was grateful for every one of those guests. Not only did they allow Eternal Rest to stay in business, but welcoming guests to her home had been a comfort to Emily since Scott's death two years ago.

These days, after being caught up in a couple of murder investigations, Eternal Rest was more popular than ever. That thought brought Emily's mind back to the present, and she said, "I still need an assistant. I can't handle all the calls and emails we're getting these days, plus do the cleaning and run errands. I have to sleep sometime!"

"I thought you were getting a new assistant?" Reed sounded surprised. "You mentioned someone coming in this week."

Emily turned her head toward Reed. "I hired someone from a temp agency to get me through this week. If I'm lucky, she'll be great, and I can offer her the job permanently. Given my recent track record, though…"

After her longtime assistant, the sweet, elderly Mrs. Thompson, had died, Emily had hired Trevor Williams. He had only been there a week when a body was discovered in a shallow grave in the cemetery next to Eternal Rest, and his dad turned out to be the one responsible for it. After that, Emily had hired Trip Ellis, who had murdered one of her guests.

It wasn't a promising trend.

I hope this temp has never even killed a fly, let alone a human being. Please let her work out.

"Em?" Sage prompted. "Yoo-hoo, where are you?" Sage leaned forward and waved a hand in front of Emily's face.

Emily blinked. "Sorry, I was thinking about assistants. The temp one starts tomorrow, which is when my guests for the week show up, so she's jumping right into it."

"Oh, I forgot to mention," said Reed, sounding slightly embarrassed. "One of your guests will be checking in early tomorrow. Kat Mason."

"She emailed me to let me know, so you're off the hook," Emily said, smiling. "I can't wait to see what the art installation looks like."

Kat was one of the artists who always stayed at Eternal Rest during the annual Oak Hill Arts Festival. This year, Kat had been invited to display an art installation at historic Hilltop Cemetery. Emily would be able to see it just by looking out her bedroom window. Kat had been secretive about the installation itself, making Emily more anxious to see it. The city of Oak Hill liked to arrange installations around town during the festival, which helped spread out the crowds of visitors a bit and showed off the town's notable spots, but this was the first time the cemetery had been put on the itinerary.

"This is one of your favorite weeks of the year," Sage said suddenly. "You've never said so, but I can feel it."

"It is," Emily said, nodding happily. "My guests every year are really cool artists, and since they're gone all day, none of them mind that I leave the house, too, to go work my volunteer shifts at the festival." Emily's smile faltered. "This is my first year hosting the artists without Mrs. Thompson here to help me."

Sage clicked her tongue impatiently. "That's not true, and you know it. She's still here to help."

"You're right." Emily lifted her eyes to the space above their heads. "Sorry, Mrs. Thompson!"

There was a loud knock on the wall as the ghost of Mrs. Thompson acknowledged Emily's apology.

Emily's stomach growled. "Want me to make dinner?" She looked at Sage and Reed expectantly.

"Jen and I are going to Morelli's tonight," Sage answered. "I helped Mrs. Morelli connect with her dead grandmother, and she gave me a gift certificate to the restaurant as a thank you."

"I can't stay, either," Reed said apologetically. "I need to be up extra early tomorrow so I can get some work done at the Garden before I come over here to meet Kat." As the sexton for the two cemeteries under the care of the city of Oak Hill, Reed had to take care of the dead at the modern (but much less interesting, in Emily's opinion) Oak Hill Memorial Garden as well as the Victorian-era Hilltop Cemetery.

Emily walked her friends onto the front porch, where she thanked them profusely for their help with the house-cleansing. They both hugged her tightly, reiterating their promises to help Scott's spirit any way they could, before getting in their cars and driving to their own homes. Emily stayed on the porch, looking at the sky, which had now turned the same hue of dark blue as Eternal Rest. She was surprised when a car on the road turned into her drive, and she raised a hand to shade her eyes from the glare of the headlights. As the car arced around the circular drive, she realized it was Sage's.

The car stopped right in front of the house, and Sage jumped out of the driver's seat. "I almost forgot!" She waved something in her hand as she skirted the car and walked up the porch steps. "Hold out your hand."

Emily complied, one eyebrow raised in question as Sage plunked a bundle into the palm of her hand. It was wrapped in bright-pink silk that exactly matched Sage's spiked hair and was tied with a white ribbon. "What's this?"

"Tarot cards. I want you to practice with them."

Emily wasn't sure whether she wanted to laugh or scoff. "Why? So I can tell fortunes at the arts festival?" she asked sarcastically.

"No. They're so much more versatile than that. Tarot cards are a great focusing and meditation tool. You can use them to help you grow your abilities."

"You mean, I can use them to communicate with ghosts?"

"Yes, but they also help you communicate with yourself, to tap into your instincts and subconscious."

"My intuition." Emily was nodding, even though she was eyeing the silk bundle doubtfully.

"Exactly."

"Thank you, but you realize I have no idea how to use these, right? Is there a user manual that comes with them?"

"Yes, of course, I put a little guide in there for you. And remember to keep them wrapped up when you're not using them. You don't want their energy getting muddled."

Emily glanced skeptically at Sage, even though she was touched by her friend's encouragement. "Noted. Thanks again, Sage."

With a wave, Sage climbed back into her car and was soon gone again. Emily stood there, feeling surprised, pleased, and a little perplexed. She had to admit Sage was right about her growing encounters with the paranormal, and maybe she really was beginning to develop the ability to interact with ghosts. If she could somehow use that budding talent to help Scott, then she appreciated every tool Sage could give her. Still, Tarot cards seemed like an odd choice. She associated them more with scarf-and-gold-hoop-laden seers than ghosts.

Once she went inside and locked the front door, Emily walked down the hallway to the kitchen and laid the silk-wrapped cards down on the antique wooden table in one corner. She untied the ribbon and unfolded the silk. The backs of the cards were printed with a beautiful but simple gold floral design that made Emily think of Art Deco style. She picked up the top card and turned it over.

It was Death.

2

Emily woke up on Tuesday morning with the same feeling of optimism that had washed over her after the house-cleansing the night before. She had felt a stab of panic when she first saw the Death card, but she had quickly consulted the sheet of paper Sage had folded up and included with the stack of Tarot cards. Sage had written some quick descriptions of each card, along with a few tips on how Emily could use them as a tool for communicating with ghosts. The Death card, Sage's guide had informed her, didn't mean a literal death, but the death of old ways and habits, and a subsequent new beginning.

It certainly felt that way to Emily this morning. Her new temp assistant would be arriving at nine for her first day at Eternal Rest, and the five artists staying there for the duration of the festival would be trickling in throughout the day. Three of them had been her guests in previous years, and she was looking forward to seeing their familiar faces.

With such thoughts in mind, Emily was showered, dressed, and sitting at her rolltop desk in the parlor by eight o'clock. She scrolled through emails and confirmed a couple of online booking requests, then spun around in her chair and gazed at the room in happy reflection. The morning sun was streaming through the windows, which Emily had cracked open to let the fresh spring air blow out any lingering sage smoke. The house smelled fine to her, but she knew that might simply be because she was used to it by now. With a contented smile, she turned back to her laptop, where another reservation request had just popped up in her email inbox.

The doorbell rang shortly before nine, and the hinges of the wooden front door creaked as Emily opened it wide to see a curvaceous woman with short blonde curls and a wide smile accented by dimples. Her hazel eyes were shining with excitement, and Emily felt her smile of politeness turn into a genuine one. Something about this woman just felt good.

Don't get ahead of yourself, Em. You liked Trip, too, and he turned out to be a killer. Don't trust anyone.

Emily actually made a waving motion, as if she could push those thoughts away. Hopefully, if this new assistant noticed, she would just think Emily was swatting at a bug.

"Hi," Emily said brightly, extending her hand. "You must be Gretchen."

"And you must be Emily," Gretchen said, shaking Emily's hand firmly. She looked like she was in her late twenties, her fitted black slacks and purple blouse giving her a look that managed to be both professional and young. "This house is beautiful! I've been to the cemetery, but I've never been this close to the house."

Emily thanked her for the compliment as she waved her inside. "Would you like some coffee?" Emily asked as she led the way into the parlor and gestured to the sofa. Gretchen readily accepted, and when Emily returned from the kitchen with two cups of coffee, milk, and sugar on a tray, she found Gretchen standing between the two front windows, looking up at a portrait of Emily's grandparents.

"They're the ones who restored the house and opened it as a bed and breakfast," Emily explained as she put the tray down. "The house was built in 1872, but my grandparents didn't buy it until 1974."

Gretchen turned to face Emily, and her smile faltered for the first time. "Is it scary living next to a cemetery?"

"No, not at all. I like to tell people I've got the best neighbors you can imagine, because they're nice and quiet."

Gretchen's eyes flicked toward the side window, which had a view of Hilltop Cemetery a few hundred feet away. "I like cemeteries in the daytime," she began. "Old ones like this have such pretty statues and carvings, and I like all the sweet things people write about each other on the headstones. I'm not sure I'd want to hang out in a cemetery at night, though."

Emily cleared her throat uncomfortably as Gretchen sat down on the sofa. Keeping a close eye on her new assistant, Emily eased down into one of the chairs and said slowly, "First, you have nothing to be afraid of out here, no matter what time of day it is. Second"—Emily paused and cleared her throat again—"I don't know what stories you've heard about Eternal Rest, but we do have some paranormal activity here."

Gretchen's eyes widened. She was stirring sugar into her coffee, and her hand froze. "I've heard the stories, but I thought they were just made up. Or, you know, embellished."

"If anyone is making the stories more dramatic than reality, then it isn't me. All you're likely to encounter here are some footsteps upstairs, or some knocking noises. Oh, and you might occasionally find words written on these sheets of paper I have sitting in each downstairs room. There's a teenage girl who haunts this place, and she likes to write. I put the pencils and paper out so she can communicate with us."

Gretchen gasped. "Is it the dead girl they found in the cemetery?"

Emily nodded, as much as she hated thinking of her newest spectral resident in that way. "Kelly Stern, yes. She's a nice girl." *As long as you're not a jerk or someone she suspects of murder.* "What about you, Gretchen? Are you from Oak Hill originally?"

Gretchen's smile returned in full force. "No, I'm from Macon. My husband is from Oak Hill, though, and we moved here two years ago. Our son is in pre-school now, so I wanted to start working again. The problem is, I don't know what I want to do! I signed up at the temp agency, so I could try different things and figure out what I'm meant to be."

Emily nodded approvingly. "That's smart. It's a good way to meet people all over town, too."

Once they both finished their coffees, Emily led Gretchen to the rolltop desk, where she went over the basics for the reservation system and told her what she could expect in terms of phone calls. "I've been flooded with calls since Kelly's murder came to light, so you'll get a lot of people wanting to book a stay. All of my guests this week are artists here for the festival, so they'll be gone all day, every day. I'll be at the festival each afternoon to volunteer, so you'll be on your own sometimes, but I think you'll get the hang of things pretty quickly."

"I'm sure I'll be fine." Gretchen reached into her purse and pulled out a small framed photo of a little boy with hazel eyes that matched hers. "Do you mind if I put this on the desk while I work? I loved being a stay-at-home mom with him, and I'll miss him now that I'm working again."

Emily nodded but stopped herself from saying anything as she felt her throat tighten. She and Scott had always talked about having kids "someday," and it was only a few months before his car crash that the two of them had seriously begun to discuss how they could run Eternal Rest and raise kids at the same time. Finally, after swallowing hard, Emily said, "What's his name?"

"Bryan Charles Robson, Jr." Gretchen was beaming.

"He's very cute. I can see why you miss seeing that face."

The doorbell rang right then, and Emily appreciated not having to stay on the subject of kids. She gestured to the desk. "You get settled in. I'll get the door."

Emily already knew it would be Kat Mason at the door, but seeing her each year was always something of a surprise. Kat was an artist, and sometimes Emily thought Kat's favorite canvas was herself. Her hair was always radically different, and her makeup was usually something bold. This year, Kat's hair was shaved on the right side of her head. Tight braids cascaded down the opposite side, spilling over her shoulder. Her yellow- and orange-hued eyeshadow set off the orange tones in her brown eyes, and she had even woven matching beads into her braids.

Before she could stop herself, Emily simply said, "Wow!"

Kat laughed and stepped forward to embrace Emily. "It's good to see you, too!" She released Emily and picked up her suitcase. "Tell me, do I have good housemates this year?"

"I sure hope so," Emily answered as they moved into the parlor. As she retrieved Kat's room key from the desk, she continued, "The Freys are staying with me again, but the other two artists are new here. I don't know why Alex didn't book a room again this year. He stayed with me for the past five festivals."

Kat's eyes widened dramatically. "You don't know? He's not on the festival circuit this year. He got a deal with a hotel chain to make art for their rooms and lobbies. I heard he's making so much money he's thinking about retiring when he's finished with the work."

"Good for him. Maybe a hotel chain will come knocking at your door, too." Emily handed over the key as Kat made a gagging sound.

"Too mainstream for me. I need to get started on this installation at the cemetery, but let's catch up tonight, okay?" Kat gave her suitcase a little shake. "I managed to squeeze in a bottle of wine I got from a client."

"You're an ideal guest," Emily said, smiling.

As Kat's footsteps retreated up the stairs, Emily turned to see Gretchen looking at her keenly. "I wanted to ask you…" she began hesitantly.

"Yes?"

"I'm sorry. I know this is a sensitive subject, but is it true that your last assistant killed one of your guests?"

"That's another story that isn't embellished." Emily rubbed her arms briskly against the sudden chill that she felt. "Yeah, Trip Ellis—his daddy owns Ellis Hardware—killed one of the investors of the old hotel outside of town. But don't worry: Jaxon was killed at the hotel, not here."

Gretchen nodded. "I saw it on the news, of course, but it just seems too strange to be true. If your last assistant hadn't murdered someone, I wouldn't be working this job right now."

Well, that's a creepy way of putting it. "That's true. And it turns out that he only asked for the job because he wanted to keep tabs on the investors. So, as long as you're here to make money and not to murder someone, I think we'll work well together."

Suddenly, Gretchen laughed self-consciously. She lowered her gaze, and Emily could see a blush creeping over her cheeks. "Sorry. I watched a lot of true-crime documentaries during Bryan's nap time each day, so I'm horrified by what that guy did, but also kind of fascinated."

"I understand. A lot of people seem to feel that way about it."

"Hey, maybe they'll make a documentary about Eternal Rest someday!"

Gretchen sounded excited at the prospect, but Emily felt a sense of dread at that idea. She wanted guests coming for the ghosts and the charming Victorian setting, not for the murders related to the house.

Of course, if it brings in more business, I can get the roof fixed...

The sound of Kat clattering excitedly down the stairs interrupted Emily's thoughts, and soon her head appeared in the parlor doorway. "I'm off to meet Reed so we can start getting set up. Wish me luck!"

"Good luck!" Emily said the words before she had a chance to wonder if Kat was referring to her art installation or to meeting up with Reed.

3

The phone started ringing shortly before ten o'clock, and Gretchen soon had her hands full taking reservations and answering questions. Eternal Rest was close to being sold out for the months of June and July already, which gave Emily more of a sense of relief than anything. When Scott had been alive, they had weathered some lean stretches, but it had never bothered Emily too much. She had always felt like everything would work out, so there was no sense in stressing about it. Without Scott by her side, though, that feeling of security had disappeared. Eternal Rest's booming business was downright soothing to Emily.

Jake and Selena Frey were the next guests to arrive, and as Emily opened the door for them, she saw a big SUV pulling in next to the Freys' utility van. Emily greeted the Freys, stepping back to let them in, and she watched over their shoulders as a middle-aged woman in a flowing black dress hopped out of the SUV. She was so short Emily wondered how she managed to get into the vehicle in the first place.

As the woman came up the steps, Emily smiled politely. "Welcome to Eternal Rest. I'm Emily."

"Hi, Emily!" The woman reached out a hand laden with two big turquoise rings. She spoke quickly, her voice deep and loud. "Marianne Callahan, sculptor. Yes, it rhymes, but it makes you remember me!"

Emily shook the woman's hand, feeling slightly overwhelmed by the artist. She wasn't worried at all about forgetting Marianne.

Once Emily got her three guests checked in and on the way upstairs to their rooms, she dashed into the kitchen to make three glasses of sweet tea for her guests. By the time she returned to the parlor, Jake and Selena were just settling onto the sofa. This was their fourth year staying at Eternal Rest during the Oak Hill Arts Festival, so they were already anticipating Emily's welcome drinks.

Emily served the tea to the Freys before sitting on the edge of one of the chairs. "How have you two been the past year?"

"Really great," Selena answered. Her long black hair hung in a braid over her shoulder, partly obscuring the words *Paint the Town* printed on it. She and Jake spent most of their year traveling to arts festivals all over the country, and last year, Selena had admitted that the only shirts she owned anymore were the souvenir ones she got at the festivals they attended. "Jake has a whole new series of paintings debuting this weekend, and I've started making painted pottery in addition to my regular work."

"Impressive! I look forward to seeing the new pieces." Emily meant it. Not all of the artists who had booths at the festival made things that suited Emily's taste, and there were a few artists whom she thought barely qualified for the title. The Freys, though, had always impressed her with their beautiful paintings. Jake mostly did country scenes, like cottages and barns, while Selena preferred more abstract designs. The two styles were wildly different from each other, but Emily could appreciate the talents of each artist.

Jake had just started to inquire after Emily when Marianne swept into the room, her deep voice raised like she was lecturing a class. "This is delightful! I was a bit skeptical about staying in a place right next to a cemetery, but this is quite nice!"

Her words were kind, but Emily felt like Marianne was shouting them at her, and it took her a moment to realize she was being paid a compliment. "Thank you," she finally said. "Please, sit down and have some tea."

Marianne took a long drink, and Jake used the opportunity to ask Emily again how she had been. "It's been a little crazy here," Emily said honestly. "I assume you heard about the murders?"

Marianne stopped drinking and stared at Emily. Jake and Selena said in unison, "Murders?"

Oh, boy. Here we go. "It's been on the news here and even in Atlanta, but I guess anyone outside of North Georgia is unlikely to have heard about them." After assuring her guests that no one had actually been murdered inside Eternal Rest, she launched into abbreviated stories about Kelly Stern and Jaxon Knight-MacGinn. Out of the corner of her eye, Emily could see Gretchen twisted around in the desk chair, listening intently.

The three artists began talking at once after Emily concluded her narrative, but it was Marianne's voice that rose above the others. "Robert Gaines posted on his social media last week that he was coming to this festival, and he said his new art delved into the dark heart of small-town life. I wonder if this is what he meant?"

Emily felt some surprise. "Robert Gaines? He stayed here during last year's festival." Emily didn't know why he hadn't booked a stay at Eternal Rest again this year, but she wasn't complaining. She had found him rather self-absorbed and shallow, and she didn't much care for his collection of altered photographs. "I doubt his new art is about the murders. It all happened really recently."

"You're probably right. I suspect his new art is about a dark heart of a different kind." Marianne sniffed derisively. "His wife is trying to wring every penny out of him in their divorce."

"So it's true, then?" Selena asked. "I'd heard he and Anita were splitting up. Frankly, I'm surprised it took this long."

Emily was startled to hear the bite in Selena's voice. Selena seemed to register Emily's reaction because she raised one hand defensively. "You've met Robert. You know he can be a little, well, full of himself. His wife is even worse. She's an artist, too, and thank goodness they usually travel different circuits. Whenever the two of them are at the same festival, it's like watching a soap opera the whole weekend. So much drama."

"I heard he's dating someone else already, so I don't think Robert is crying into his cognac every night," Jake added.

"He and that beaded jewelry maker are probably at the local bar already, trying to pick up women," Marianne said disapprovingly.

Emily giggled, and it quickly turned into hearty laughter. At the strange look from her guests, she took a moment to calm herself down before saying, "Sorry, I know it's not funny, but it sounds like the festival community gossips every bit as much as people here in Oak Hill. Your world seems so different than mine, yet it's so similar."

Jake looked at Emily grimly, but his eyes were shining with humor. "Maybe Marianne is right: Robert's new art is about the dark heart of small-town life, but the small town just so happens to be our own artists' community."

The fifth and final guest of the week arrived at four o'clock. By that time, Jake, Selena, and Marianne had already gone downtown to check in at the arts festival. Gretchen was still busy fielding calls, and Emily was seated at the dining room table with a polishing cloth and the silverware she had inherited from her grandparents.

When Emily had seen the name Gregory Van Breda pop up on Eternal Rest's online reservation system, she had gotten a very clear idea in her head of what an artist with such a name might look like. She pictured someone rich, who painted not to make money but simply for something to do with all of his privileged time, and she imagined one pinky sticking out daintily as he held a watercolor brush.

The real Gregory Van Breda looked nothing like what Emily had imagined. In fact, he seemed to be the complete opposite of Marianne Callahan in every way. Where she had a tiny body but a giant personality and voice, Gregory towered over Emily, his wide shoulders filling up the doorway, but he spoke in a voice so quiet Emily had to lean forward slightly to hear him. Gregory's dirty-blond hair hung down to his shoulders, and he ran a hand nervously through it as Emily introduced herself.

"You must be Gregory," she said. "Welcome to Eternal Rest."

"Just Greg is fine," he said softly as Emily's hand nearly disappeared into his.

This is what it feels like to shake hands with a giant.

As Emily led Greg into the parlor and retrieved his room key, she wondered if he would even fit in his bed. She was certain he was the tallest guest to ever stay at Eternal Rest. *Maybe I should start a wall of fame. Tallest guest, oldest guest, guest who committed the most murders…*

After Emily handed Greg his key and gave him instructions to simply turn right at the top of the stairs, she asked, "What kind of art do you make?"

"I'm a sculptor."

"Oh! Then I have two sculptors at Eternal Rest this week. Marianne Callahan is staying here, too."

Greg's eyebrows rose ever so slightly, and one side of his mouth curved up. Emily thought he looked like he hadn't smiled in so long that he had forgotten how to do it properly. "Marianne and I have very different styles," Greg said quietly.

Emily couldn't tell if Greg was being critical of his fellow sculptor or simply stating a fact, so she responded politely, "Then I look forward to seeing work by both of you when I'm at the festival this week."

Greg declined Emily's offer of iced tea, and soon he had disappeared upstairs, leaving Emily feeling mystified. Over the years, she had learned to quickly get a sense of whether or not someone was going to be an agreeable guest. Greg Van Breda felt like a giant question mark in Emily's mind.

Emily was still mulling over her latest guest a short time later, when she looked at the clock and realized it was time to get ready to head into downtown Oak Hill for the arts festival volunteer meeting. Gretchen had agreed to work a little late that night, so the artists wouldn't come home to an empty house.

As she made the drive into town, Emily could see signs of the coming festival everywhere. Businesses sponsoring the event had stuck signs in their front lawns or hung them in the windows, announcing they were a proud supporter of the Oak Hill Arts Festival. Banners had been hung from the old-fashioned streetlights in the area around the square, which was in the middle of the historic district and the heart of Oak Hill.

Emily parked a couple blocks away, since traffic was already being diverted from the streets around the square. As she walked, she could see the rows of white vinyl tents set up for each artist's booth, and Emily felt her anticipation growing. As much as she enjoyed looking at the art each year, Emily knew one of the reasons she loved the festival so much was because it allowed her to get out of Eternal Rest every day. Ordinarily, she would be stuck there waiting for guests to check in or hanging around in case they came back early. This was the one week that both Emily and her guests were all out of the house, doing the same thing.

The volunteers were meeting around the white gazebo that sat in the middle of the square. The gazebo was covered in party lights and gold bunting for the festival. As Emily threaded her way toward the crowd already gathered there, she could sense an anxious sort of atmosphere. A number of volunteers were standing in a loose circle to one side of the gazebo, all bent at the waist and looking down at something.

One of the women in the group looked up, her face angry. Emily gasped as she recognized Trish from Grainy Day Bakery. Trish was usually full of energy and gossip, and Emily had seen her fired up but never truly angry. Trish's eyes met Emily's, and Emily found her feet leading her toward the group, even while her brain told her not to get involved in whatever was happening.

A young woman was sitting on the ground in the middle of the circle, crying. She was running her fingers through her wavy brown hair over and over again, which was frizzed from the motions.

Emily edged her way around the group until she was standing just behind Trish. "What's happening? Does she need medical help?" Emily kept her voice low.

Trish straightened up and turned to face Emily. Her thick Southern accent was tinged with malice. "What she needs is for someone to go tell that artist Robert Gaines that it's not okay to humiliate people in our town."

Emily's eyes flicked down to the woman, who was now being helped to her feet by a couple of people. She was still sniffling and taking shaky breaths.

"What did he do?" Emily asked.

"Jess went by Robert's booth while he was setting up. You know he takes photographs, then does stuff to them?" Trish said the words like he was doing something indecent, and she kept her voice low. "Well, apparently, he met Jess last year and asked her to model for him. They took pictures around town, and she said it was cute stuff. Nothing, you know, risqué. Today, Jess sees one of the photos up on the wall of Robert's booth, but he'd completely changed it. Jess's body was covered in magazine clippings of half-dressed women, so she looks like some kind of Frankenstein's Lady of the Night."

Emily was stunned, and her mind went right back to the conversation with her guests about Robert's new series of art depicting the dark heart of small-town life. She wondered how many other pieces were in the collection, and how many other people were going to be embarrassed in such a public way. "Poor girl," Emily said softly. "Can't she ask him to take it down?"

Trish waved Emily after her as she stepped away from the crowd. "That's the worst part. She signed a release giving him permission to use the photos in his art. Of course, she never expected he would twist the images into something so distasteful. You can't really tell it's her in the photo, because almost every inch of her has been covered with the clippings. She recognized herself, of course, but hopefully no one else will. We've been trying to convince her of that, but every time she walks by that booth this week, she's going to know, and right now, that's all that matters to her. Bless her heart." Trish's voice had been getting faster and louder as she spoke, and Emily could feel the anger rolling off her friend. Like Jess, Trish's hair was disheveled, like she had been tugging at her blonde French braid in frustration.

"He stayed at Eternal Rest last year," Emily said. "I don't know why he didn't come back this year, but I'm really happy he didn't. It's about time the latest scandal didn't revolve around my house."

"It's not about one business or another. It's about the whole town. The photo was taken right in front of City Hall. I'm sure it was adorable before Robert got *artistic*"— Trish's fingers stabbed angrily as she made air quotes— "with it. What's he trying to say about Oak Hill? He comes into our town and wants to get money by making us look like a laughing stock?"

Emily often thought Trish overreacted to bad news and scandalous gossip. She had a tendency to get riled up about things Emily just didn't think were that big of a deal, but this time, she could understand her friend's anger. Robert Gaines hadn't just humiliated Jess, but everyone who took pride in their small town.

Trish gave her head a little shake and changed the subject. "Before I start yelling, let's talk about something else. Have you seen the installation at the cemetery yet?"

"No. Kat Mason is the artist, and she's been out there all day setting up. I don't know if she and Reed will finish up tonight, or if she'll still be working on it tomorrow. I've also got two new artists staying with me this year: both sculptors."

"That's a coincidence," Trish noted, but already her attention was drifting away as someone climbed the steps of the gazebo and grabbed a microphone attached to a portable speaker.

"Good evening, festival volunteers!" It was Jen Clark, Sage's wife. Working with the festival was part of her job at the Oak Hill Chamber of Commerce. Emily was sure Sage would get an earful about Robert Gaines from Jen, who took anything that cast Oak Hill in a bad light as not just a personal affront, but a professional one, too.

"Thank you for coming out tonight, and of course, thank you so much for volunteering your time, energy, and talent to the Oak Hill Arts Festival this week!" Jen was smiling broadly. Her red hair was pulled up in a high bun, and her tailored slacks and blouse showed off her small frame. "You should have all received a copy of the volunteer schedule yesterday by email. If not, let me know afterward, and I'll give you a physical copy."

Emily only half paid attention as Jen continued. She kept turning slightly to glance at Jess. Emily didn't know her, but she guessed Jess was somewhere in her early twenties. It was easy to see why Robert had wanted her to model for him: she was an attractive girl, even with mascara under her eyes and a red, puffy face from crying. A man about the same age as Jess had his arm around her comfortingly, and as Emily watched, someone brought Jess a bottle of water and pushed it into her hand.

Emily smiled grimly to herself. Robert Gaines was going to have a very long week at the Oak Hill Arts Festival. She wondered how many snide remarks he would hear from upset locals.

The people around Emily suddenly began to applaud.

Startled, Emily joined in, realizing that Jen had wrapped up the meeting. As people began turning to each other and the buzz of chatter grew, Emily felt a hand on her shoulder. She turned to find herself looking right into the bright-blue eyes of Trevor Williams.

Trevor smiled shyly. "Hi, Emily. You're volunteering, too? I guess you got a new assistant to watch things at Eternal Rest."

"Hey, Trevor." Things still felt a little awkward between her and her former assistant, but still, Emily was genuinely happy to see him. She liked Trevor, and she felt like they could be friends, if only they could get over the lingering discomfort. Kelly Stern's ghost had violently attacked Trevor because she mistook him for her killer. Since the actual murderer turned out to be Trevor's dad, Emily knew it would take a while before she and Trevor could just act normal with each other. "I hired someone from a temp agency to help out this week. How about you? Are you diving into community events so soon after moving back to Oak Hill?"

Trevor smiled. "My company does all the graphic design for the festival. They gave us a choice this week of either being in the office or volunteering here. I'd much rather be outside enjoying myself, even if it means telling lost tourists where the porta-potties are."

"You'll have fun, I promise. We still need to get together for coffee. It's been a little crazy for me lately, but I feel like that can't be an excuse anymore. If it's not one thing, it's another, so I just need to make time so we can catch up."

"As long as it's not more dead bodies clogging up your schedule," Trevor said, deadpan.

If he's able to crack a joke at his own dad's expense, then I guess he's working through the mental trauma of it all.

"It actually is because of the dead bodies," Emily

admitted. "The phone is ringing constantly. I always get a lot of ghost hunters, but I've got even more groups calling now because they want to communicate with Kelly. I don't even know how they're finding out that her ghost decided to stay at Eternal Rest, but it's really helping business."

"That's a little weird for me but good for you," Trevor said. "Back to coffee. What's your schedule this week? Maybe we can meet up before or after a shift."

"I'm working each afternoon. You?"

"All day, every day. Again, it beats being at my desk. I get breaks, though, so how about Thursday, before the afternoon volunteer shift starts? Most people will wait for the weekend to attend, so we should be able to find a spot at The Stomping Grounds pretty easily."

"Deal! I look forward to it."

Trevor smiled at Emily as he ran a hand self-consciously through his dark hair. "Have a good night. I'm sure I'll see you out here tomorrow."

Emily wished him a good night, and as soon as he was out of earshot, she felt an elbow against her ribs.

"Did you just make a date with Trevor Williams?" Trish's eyes were comically wide.

"No, of course not! You know I don't date anybody. We're just going to catch up. He needs friends, Trish."

"Mmm-hmm. I'll see you tomorrow. I've got to get home before my husband decides to take a stab at making dinner. The last time was a disaster." Trish gave Emily a little wave as she disappeared through a cluster of volunteers.

Emily spent the entire drive home worried that she had accidentally made a date with Trevor. *No, he knows it's not like that. Right?*

Emily walked through her front door only to be pounced on by Kat, who must have been in the parlor and heard her coming. Kat grabbed Emily by the shoulders and yelled, "It's going to look amazing, Emily!"

"The installation?"

"Yes! We didn't get it all set up yet, but what we did get done is looking so good! Reed was an absolute saint today, though I finally had to promise to buy him dinner to get him to do a little last-minute landscaping for me around one of the mausoleums."

Emily nodded knowingly. "Food is always a good way to get Reed to do something." She almost teased Kat about making dinner plans with him, then caught herself. She didn't want to risk making Kat feel as uncomfortable as Trish had made her feel such a short while before. Instead, she said, "Where are you two going?"

"Reed swears that the best barbecue is one town over. I told him to prove it. Oh! Oh no, Emily, I said I'd hang out with you tonight! Do you mind putting off our wine and catch-up?"

"Not a problem," Emily reassured her. If Emily was honest with herself, she was actually rather relieved. Bed was sounding a lot more attractive than wine at the moment. "You two have a nice time."

Kat had walked out the front door and shut it behind her before Emily realized she was still standing in the hallway with her purse dangling from her shoulder. She began to make a beeline for her bedroom, then remembered her assistant was still working.

Emily found Gretchen sitting at the desk in the parlor, writing in a small spiral notebook. As Emily dropped her purse unceremoniously on the sofa, Gretchen looked up. "Hi, Emily. It's been a busy day. Eternal Rest is now sold out for the month of July."

"That's fantastic! Thank you, Gretchen. Did you have any problems today?"

"No, just lots of phone calls."

"Did any of the ghosts come say hello?"

Gretchen actually looked disappointed as she answered in the negative. "But," she added hopefully, "maybe they just need to get used to me!"

"Maybe you're so competent that Mrs. Thompson doesn't think you need her help. She used to have your job."

"She died?"

Emily just nodded, and Gretchen gasped. "So, one of your assistants died before another one turned out to be a murderer?"

Emily decided not to mention Trevor's brief stint as her assistant in between those two. If she did, Gretchen might think the position was cursed. Instead, she said, "Mrs. Thompson was a retired widow. She died from plain old age, so no one is going to make a true crime documentary about her. You can head on home. Go enjoy some time with your son, and I'll see you tomorrow."

"Okay. Thank you, Emily. I enjoyed my first day."

"Thank you, Gretchen."

Soon, Emily was alone in the house, and she figured the rest of her guests, like Kat, were out having dinner at a restaurant. Emily wasted no time in making herself a quick dinner and scarfing it down at the table in the kitchen. When she was finally full, she sat back with a sigh. It was a little too early for bed. Instead, she retrieved the Tarot cards from her bedroom and returned to the kitchen. She unwrapped the bundle and stopped to look at Sage's instructions. It was pretty straightforward: Emily should ask to communicate with one of the ghosts at Eternal Rest, and the ghost would—allegedly—help Emily's hand choose the right card to match its message.

Emily felt skeptical about the idea. She didn't doubt Sage's ability to communicate with ghosts, and she had certainly had her own paranormal encounters, but trying to figure out what a ghost wanted to say by looking at a picture on a card seemed deceptively simple. Emily figured hundreds of people could look at one card, and every one of them would interpret it differently.

With an indifferent shrug, Emily began to shuffle the deck. *Not like you'd shuffle playing cards,* Sage had written. *Be gentle!* Sage had also instructed Emily to call out to the ghost she wanted to communicate with. Kelly was the one who had alerted Emily to the fact that Scott's spirit had not yet crossed over, but she hadn't given any details beyond that. As Emily carefully shuffled the cards, she called out, "Kelly, are you here? Sage has an interesting new way for us to communicate. You can help me choose the right card for your message. These cards all have meanings, but you can also choose based on the picture. Do you want to try this with me? I want you to help me pick a card!"

Emily closed her eyes as her hands slowed. She wasn't sure what she was supposed to be feeling, but suddenly, some strong emotion stabbed through her. It felt less like guidance from a teenage ghost and more like a warning. Emily took a deep breath as she pressed her palm against the top card. Was she feeling fear? Anxiety? No, it felt more like urgency, like something was trying to prod her into motion. Emily's heart picked up its pace, and a slight chill passed through her as her adrenaline spiked.

Emily took another deep breath, opened her eyes, and turned over the card. It was Justice. As she sat there looking at it, she heard the front door open and close with a bang, and the sound of several pairs of feet on the stairs.

Calm down. It's just some of your guests.

The sense of urgency was still strong, but Emily forced herself to sit back. Finally, she began to relax. "What does this have to do with Scott?" she asked to the empty kitchen.

Unsettled by the feeling that had come over her, Emily re-wrapped the cards and returned them to their spot in her nightstand drawer. *Maybe,* she thought, *I'm not quite ready for this kind of spirit communication.*

Emily had spent a restless night in bed, dreaming about footsteps walking up to her bedroom door. Every time, Emily would open the door to find herself face-to-face with a judge in a long black robe, who sneered as he raised one arm to point at her in accusation.

When Emily put breakfast out at seven o'clock Wednesday morning, she could hear movement above her and hoped her guests had spent a more restful night than she had. They would all be putting the finishing touches on their booths throughout the morning, and that afternoon was what the Chamber of Commerce called the "Art Lovers' Sneak Peek." Attendees could pay a fee to get early access to the festival, giving them the chance to see and buy the art first.

Emily's guests began drifting downstairs half an hour later. By then, Emily was settled in at her desk, a coffee cup steaming away next to her laptop. Marianne bustled into the room, her purple skirt whirling around her ankles as she said, "Good morning! My booth is all set up, so I'm going to go take a look at this cemetery of yours. Where are the best sculptures?" Even to Emily, who was a morning person, a voice speaking so loudly that early in the day was jarring.

Emily wondered if Marianne ever slowed down, or if she just had an off button that she pressed when normal people went to sleep at night. "The cemetery has ring paths around the hill," she answered. "The top ring paths are mostly mausoleums, so you might want to stick to the second and third paths up for good statues and carved headstones."

Marianne expressed her thanks, and even that managed to sound aggressive. Emily really wanted to see Marianne and Trish together: two tiny women who could plow over anyone in their way with just their personalities. Emily actually snorted as she suppressed a laugh at the vision, hoping Marianne didn't hear it as she turned and left the parlor.

Greg was the last guest to leave, nursing his coffee in the dining room for a long time as he gazed out the front windows. Emily had gone in to clean up the dishes and trays, not even realizing he was still there. She actually jumped when she caught sight of him. Whether he was brooding or just enjoying some quiet time before a busy day, Emily couldn't tell.

"Oh, sorry!" Emily said as Greg glanced at her. "I thought everyone was gone."

"There is no need to apologize," Greg said softly. He paused, and his eyebrows drew together. "Perhaps I am the one who should apologize, though. I sometimes scare people."

"I can't imagine why," Emily said, keeping her voice

even. *I mean, you're a mysterious giant, but you're more unsettling than scary.*

Greg gave a little shrug. "People talk a lot. I don't. It makes them uncomfortable. Some of these artists"—Greg waved vaguely—"they don't know when to stop talking."

There was a strange tone in Greg's voice, and Emily asked cautiously, "Has one of the other artists here said something unkind to you?"

"To me? No. I don't mean that. I mean art should speak for itself."

Emily tried to find a polite response for that, finally settling for a simple, "Yes, it should."

"True art should be unexpected. It should make you think. You shouldn't have to explain yourself to anyone." Apparently taking his own advice, Greg raised his coffee cup to his lips and returned his gaze to the window.

6

It was nearly nine when Greg finally left, and Emily had just finished loading the dishwasher with the final breakfast dishes when the doorbell rang. Normally, she would give her assistant a key to Eternal Rest, but since Gretchen was only there for the week, it didn't seem worth it. In fact, Emily had to remind herself, she had never gotten her keys back from Trevor or Trip. Trevor would be easy; she would just ask him for it when they met on Thursday. Trip's key was probably in some evidence bag at the police station.

Gretchen had a smile on her face again this morning when she arrived, and her green silk blouse shimmered as Emily warmly welcomed her inside. "Sorry I'm late," Gretchen said breathlessly, holding up a small paper bag. "I had to stop by the pharmacy. My father-in-law is diabetic."

"You're not late at all! I hope you came hungry." After Emily offered her coffee and some Grainy Day Bakery leftovers from breakfast, Gretchen settled in at the desk with a bagel.

Emily got the guest rooms tidied, and by ten thirty, she had nothing left to do. She felt restless, and she guessed it was a leftover feeling from the unexpected urgency that had surged through her during the Tarot card experience the night before. The feeling was uncomfortable because

Emily didn't know if it was coming from her own mind, or if she had somehow channeled the emotion from a ghost. Had something been trying to communicate with her? Had Scott been trying to tell her that he needed urgent help? If that were the case, then Emily still had no idea how to even reach him, let alone help him. There was nothing she could do.

Fighting off a rising feeling of helplessness, Emily decided to head into Oak Hill, even though her volunteer shift wouldn't begin until one o'clock. She could start learning where the various artists were located and stop by Jake and Selena's booth to see their new pieces. Plus, she had promised to drop off a few Eternal Rest T-shirts for the festival's raffle.

Gretchen had already booked two reservations by the time Emily left, and June was on track to be sold out by the end of the week. During the drive into downtown Oak Hill, Emily dreamed of the new roof she was going to get as she tried to decide what color shingles would look best on the house.

Since Oak Hill High School was closed for spring break, the teacher parking lot had been cordoned off for volunteer parking during the festival. It was a two-block walk from the school to the square, and Emily enjoyed the warm sunshine. Her Oak Hill Arts Festival volunteer T-shirt was a shocking lime-green color, and Emily felt like she must be a distraction to every driver who passed her as she walked along the sidewalk.

When Emily arrived at the square, she skirted the outside of the cluster of booths until she reached the registration tent. She found Jen in there, talking quickly into a cell phone. Jen's eyes met Emily's, and she held up a finger. Emily chatted conversationally with a few of the other volunteers until Jen stuffed her phone into her pocket with a huff and marched up to Emily. "Artists." Jen spoke quietly, but she spit out the word.

Emily just laughed. "Let me guess: you've got a high-maintenance Michelangelo?"

"You know those horror stories about couples trying to assign seating for their wedding receptions? 'Cousin So-and-so can't sit next to Uncle You-know-who, and all of our parents are divorced and can't sit at the same table as their exes…' Well, artists can be just as bad when it comes to assigning booths. I love this festival, but I love it a lot more once it actually starts. People are less demanding when they're making money."

"Well, I just came by to give things away." Emily held up the shopping bag she carried in one hand. "These are the Eternal Rest shirts for the raffle."

Jen thanked Emily as she took the bag. "I have to get going," she added, rolling her eyes. "I've got an oil painter who refuses to be next door to a folk artist, because that's not what he calls 'real' art. Seriously, Emily, we can trade places if you want."

"I'm perfectly happy with my job and my guests, thank you very much." Emily watched as Jen hustled away, and as she began to turn toward the nearby volunteer tent, she felt a light tap on her shoulder. She turned around and saw Roger Newton. It was the first time Emily had seen him wearing something other than his Oak Hill Police Department uniform. She guessed he was somewhere in his mid-fifties, but the gray T-shirt he was wearing showed that his stocky frame was mostly muscle. "Officer Newton, it's good to see you!"

"Hi, Miss Emily. I see you're volunteering, too."

Emily looked at him quizzically. "You make it sound like you're a volunteer, but you're not wearing the required glow-in-the-dark shirt. I didn't see you at the meeting last night, either."

"I help out the festival security team when I'm off-duty. We're supposed to blend in, not be visible from space."

"I still owe you coffee and biscuits so we can have a little chat about ghosts," Emily said, remembering her most recent encounter with Roger. *Yet another coffee date to make good on.*

Roger glanced away. "Ah, that's okay. I... I'm sure there's a logical explanation for what happened out at that place."

Emily knew her disappointment showed on her face. Roger, who was a skeptic about ghosts, had experienced two very paranormal things at the crumbling Mountain View Manor. Emily had promised to discuss it with him, but Trip had been arrested shortly after, and in the aftermath, Emily had simply forgotten all about it. "Officer Newton, you witnessed things that a lot of ghost hunters would be thrilled about. If it wasn't ghosts drawing in the dust or stomping around, then what was it?"

"I don't know. Some kind of animal, maybe. Leaving tracks that just looked like drawings to you. Making noises inside the hotel lobby." Roger at least had the decency to look embarrassed at such lame attempts to explain away the ghostly activity. He and Emily both knew that an animal couldn't have accidentally spelled out her name in the dusty lobby floor.

"If you ever change your mind, then there's a Basket Full of Biscuits with your name on it," Emily said encouragingly. Tempting Roger with one of the most popular specials at Trish's bakery might not convince him ghosts were real, but at least it might get a conversation going.

"Thanks. By the way, did you hear that we found your murdered guest's car?"

"Jaxon's BMW? No, I hadn't heard that."

"Just a couple days ago. Trip had stashed it in an old gravel pit about five miles outside of town. He must have walked home afterward, but he didn't leave a single fingerprint on it. He hid his tracks well. If you hadn't figured it out and wrung that confession from him, he'd probably still be a free man."

And still working for me. Emily shivered despite the warmth of the day. "I'm glad I could help," was all she said in response. Of course, it was the ghosts of Mountain View Manor and even the ghost of Jaxon himself who had led her to the truth, but since Roger was back to his skeptical ways, Emily figured there was no point in mentioning them.

Emily said goodbye to Roger and continued wandering. She still had plenty of time before her shift began, and even though she wanted to grab a quick lunch beforehand, Emily decided to start at one side of the square and work her way down every single row of booths. Most of the artists were already set up, or very close to it, so she could take a look at all of the art without the crowds that would be there during the weekend.

Jake and Selena were on the second row, and as Emily walked up, Jake waved an arm grandly. "Welcome to my new collection!"

Emily gasped and clapped her hands with delight. "Jake! These are wonderful!" The six oil paintings hanging from a rusted piece of fencing, which Jake had converted into a makeshift display wall, all depicted scenes around Oak Hill. Two of the historic mansions near the outer edges of downtown were there, as was a barn that everyone in Oak Hill simply called The Barn, because its dilapidated state made it an easy landmark when giving directions. Sutter's Bar looked quaint against a backdrop of pine trees, and the historic downtown was represented by City Hall and the old brick firehouse.

Jake was beaming with pride as Emily said, "I'm sure everyone else is as thrilled as I am."

"I've sold two of them already, and the show isn't even open yet! I took photos of these places last year, so I could paint them. I actually did this for a couple of other festivals we visit. Not surprisingly, people love seeing their own town represented." Jake nodded toward the other side of the booth. "Of course, Selena is going to be my toughest competition this weekend."

Selena was bent over a large cardboard box, her head and shoulders lost in its depths. Her voice echoed as she responded, "The loser has to load the van on Sunday night!"

Emily was admiring Selena's painted pottery when she heard a triumphant shout.

"I found it!" Selena straightened up and opened her hand. In her palm was the tiniest pottery bowl Emily had ever seen. "It's a little bird feeder," Selena explained, extending her hand toward Emily. The inside of the bowl had been painted with the finest of brush strokes, the lines forming a bird's head and beak.

"Of course, I can't make many of these," Selena continued. "I'd go blind if I had to paint lots of these little things, but I thought it would be cute on someone's windowsill."

"Definitely." Emily praised both Jake and Selena's latest pieces some more before continuing on her way, feeling a sense of pride that her guests were so talented.

Emily was still smiling as she made the turn onto the next row, but the first piece of art she saw made her stop abruptly. Even from ten feet away, Emily recognized Eternal Rest.

But her home didn't look like a piece of art. It looked like the setting for a horror movie.

Emily had to blink a few times as she stared at such a distorted depiction of her home. Slowly, she walked toward the piece, thinking perhaps she had simply gotten the wrong first impression. Maybe she wasn't looking at it the right way. But with every step forward, she felt her anger growing as she realized she wasn't mistaken. It was a photo of Eternal Rest, but it had been altered.

An altered photograph. Emily glanced up at the sign hanging from the top of the tent, but she already knew it was the name Robert Gaines there. When he had told Marianne that his new work would be about the dark heart of small-town life, he hadn't just meant the altered photo of Jess. He had also been talking about Eternal Rest.

The photo of the house had been darkened so the blue of the clapboard siding appeared almost black. The third-floor window had what looked like a piece of a book page pasted in its middle. The rough-edged scrap of paper had a ghost printed on it. This wasn't a friendly-looking apparition but one caught in a never-ending scream. The other windows were populated with similar suffering figures, as well as something that looked vaguely like a zombie.

The rest of the photo was just as horrifying. The landscape around Eternal Rest, which Emily had always thought of as beautiful and peaceful, had been made to look frightening, with dark tones, human-shaped shadows peeking out from behind tree trunks, and storm clouds looming menacingly over everything. Hilltop Cemetery hadn't been left out, either, as it reared up behind the house like a monster. The real Hilltop sat to the right of Eternal Rest, so Emily knew that a photo of Hilltop must have been digitally added to the photo of the house. The hill the cemetery sat on had been manipulated to look steeper than it actually was, and a host of ghosts and dark figures were streaming down its sides.

Emily just stood there for a full minute, staring at such an awful version of Eternal Rest. Her anger increased with every second, but there was another emotion that she couldn't quite pinpoint. It almost felt like embarrassment.

Out of the corner of her eye, she saw Robert as he walked up to her. His tanned face and gray eyes looked smug as he said, "Brand new for this year. Showing off the darkness that lives even here in Oak Hill. Maybe you don't know all of this town's wicked secrets."

Emily thought he sounded like a slimy salesman trying to convince her to pay a premium price for a broken-down car. She actually felt the fingers of her right hand curl into a fist. Never in her life had she wanted to punch someone square in the nose. Right in the middle of his smiling, self-satisfied face.

Finally, with an effort, Emily turned her eyes from the photo to the artist, though she wasn't sure this new view was any less horrifying. "That's my house," she said through clenched teeth.

"Oh." Awareness crept across Robert's face, but his smile never faltered. "Oh, yeah. I remember you. I took the photo while I was staying there last year. How do you feel about your place being featured in my art?"

Emily swallowed as she thought about what to say. It wouldn't be worth making a scene, she knew, and the last thing she wanted to do was create a rift between the volunteers and the artists. She could just imagine Jen's face if Robert went to her with a complaint about Emily. Eventually, she simply answered, "Eternal Rest is a welcoming place. It's nothing like you make it look."

"But that's just the thing, isn't it? It seems welcoming to an outsider, but you say that place is haunted. You have thousands of dead people next door. You might tell people it's a cute little bed and breakfast, but this"—Robert spread his arms as if he might actually embrace the photo—"this shows the truth. That's what art is, of course. It shows the truth of things. The darkness lying under the sweet exterior. The rotten heart of a little town."

"Stop." Emily's voice was just a whisper. "Just stop."

She wanted to say more. She wanted to tell Robert how wrong he was, how offended she was that he could ever look at the house she had dedicated her life to—that her grandparents had gone to so much effort to restore and beautify—and see tortured souls and storm clouds.

That ghost's agonized expression, peering through the window of the gabled room like it was trapped, made her think of Scott's spirit, asking for help. But so far, Emily hadn't been able to help. No one knew how to find Scott's spirit, let alone help him.

A little noise escaped Emily's lips as she turned and walked as quickly as she could in the opposite direction. She wanted to run, but there was still that little rational voice in her head that told her to stay calm and not make a scene. Still, she couldn't help the tears that started running down her cheeks. She put her head down and kept her eyes on the grass as she continued walking.

Where can I go? Where can I get away from everyone before I can't hold it in anymore?

Suddenly, a hand shot out and latched itself firmly around Emily's forearm. Emily looked at the hand in surprise, but she recognized the silver wedding ring, and she simply kept her head down and let Sage lead her along.

Sage stopped and let go of Emily's arm as soon as they were inside a tent. As Emily finally raised her head, she saw Sage yanking closed a beaded purple curtain that was hanging across the middle of the tent, cutting off the world outside.

"Sit." Sage was pointing at one of the folding chairs situated around a small circular table, which was covered with a deep-red cloth that had gold fringe along the edges.

Emily sat and buried her face in her hands. She opened her mouth to tell Sage what had happened, but a sob came out instead. Emily gave in and let the tears flow, and she felt Sage leaning over her shoulders, her arms wrapped tightly around Emily.

Sage remained silent, seeming to know that Emily just needed to let out all of the emotion. It had been months since she had cried this hard over Scott, and she was surprised how raw her emotions were even two years after his death.

Emily knew Sage's psychic abilities were at work when she said soothingly, "You're not still grieving for his death. You're grieving again because we don't know how to help his spirit."

With a last little sniff, Emily finally sat up, wiping at her cheeks with her fingers. "You're right," she croaked.

Sage retrieved a bottle of water from somewhere and took off the cap before handing it to Emily. As Emily took a long drink, Sage said, "What prompted this? Did something happen with the Tarot cards?"

Emily looked up at Sage, astonished. "Didn't you see it? That awful piece of so-called art?"

Sage's eyes narrowed. "No. I just saw you walking like a drunk person down the row."

"Robert Gaines, the artist who upset that volunteer so much? He didn't just humiliate her. He alters photos to twist people and places into these awful things. Sage, he made Eternal Rest look like, like..." Emily buried her face in her hands again.

Sage made soothing noises as she rubbed Emily's back. "It's okay. Let me guess. He took a photo of your house but altered it to make it look spooky?"

"That's putting it lightly," Emily mumbled between her fingers.

"You're used to dealing with skeptics. If someone wants to take things to the extreme opposite direction, depicting Eternal Rest as an evil place, then you can deal with that, too. You and your guests know the ghosts aren't scary or dangerous, and that's all that matters."

Emily sat up again, took a long drink of water, and swallowed hard. "You've got a point. You deal with people who think you're evil because you're a psychic medium. I'm sure there are people who think me being so open and accepting of the paranormal is just as bad, but I've never had them confront me the way people have confronted you. How do you deal with it?"

"I ignore them." Sage moved to the other chair and sat down. "It's hard at first, but you have to remember that people will always judge you. If it's someone you don't even know—"

"Robert stayed at Eternal Rest last year."

"Okay, if it's someone you barely know, remember that their opinions are both out of your control and not your concern. It takes time to learn how to ignore the haters, but you can do it."

Emily nodded slowly as she thought. "You're right, of course. Though, for me, it's about more than just one artist's opinion. Thousands of people come to this festival. I don't want them all looking at my house in that way!"

"Most of those thousands of people won't even know it's Eternal Rest. Those who do recognize the house, know it's not like that."

"Yeah, just like everyone told Jess. She knows it's her in the art, but no one else will know it."

Sage's eyes narrowed. "Jen told me about what happened at the volunteer meeting last night. She said that next year, when artists submit their applications for the festival, his will probably get lost. Accidentally, of course."

"Good. He can go paint horrible versions of someone else's house." For the first time since Sage had led here there, Emily finally looked around the tent she was sitting in. "Is this your booth?"

"Of course. I put the curtain up so that when I consult with someone, they have some privacy."

Emily had been excited when Sage announced she would have a booth at the festival. Every year, there were a few spots reserved for local businesses, even though they had nothing to do with art. Emily had expressed her doubt that Sage would be able to communicate with ghosts in the middle of such a crowded, noisy place, but Sage had assured her it wouldn't be a problem.

A floor lamp was in one corner of the little curtained space they were sitting in now, and it had a red bulb in it. A strand of tiny golden lights hung from the top of the tent, arcing gracefully over the table. Sage had taken pains to create the right ambience, right down to the large rug that covered the grass.

"It looks really great, Sage. I hope you get a lot of business this week."

"Me, too! Maybe this artist guy will come by, and I can tell him that all of his ancestors are just shaking their heads in disbelief at his terrible work."

Emily laughed softly. "Thanks for rescuing me."

"Anytime."

"Speaking of time," Emily began, looking at her watch. "Oh, it's only noon. I still have a whole hour before my shift." Earlier, the idea of grabbing a quick lunch at one of the restaurants around the square had sounded delightful. Now, it sounded lonely. Suddenly struck with an idea, Emily stood quickly. "I'm going to the cemetery."

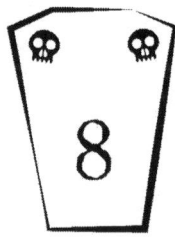

Sage smiled knowingly at Emily. "I think a visit with Scott is a good idea." She rummaged around in a small cooler sitting near her on the rug, then pulled out a sandwich. "I brought this with me, but Jen dropped off some food from the staff lunch, so you can have it. You can tell Scott what a delicious chicken salad sandwich I made."

"I will." Emily leaned over and kissed the top of Sage's head. "Thanks again. Good luck with the early birds today!"

The sunshine seemed even brighter after being in the dimness of the tent, and its warmth felt reassuring to Emily. She wasted no time walking back to her car and driving to Oak Hill Memorial Garden, which was just a couple miles outside of town. She knew she wouldn't have much time, but even a few minutes would help soothe her after such an emotional experience.

Emily parked her car at the side of the narrow road that wound through Oak Hill's modern cemetery and made the short walk to Scott's grave. She had always found the Garden, as Reed called it, rather boring. While Hilltop had mausoleums, statues, large carved headstones, and plenty of full-grown trees, the Garden was really more of a lawn. The green grass stretched over a wide, flat area, and there were only a few trees and shrubs here and there. The headstones were, for the most part, simple ones that sat flush with the ground. Eternal Rest had been closed to burials for the past thirty years, when Oak Hill City Council decided that new bodies should go in the new cemetery. Otherwise, Emily would have insisted on burying Scott at Hilltop Cemetery. Not only would he have been right next door to her, but he would have been laid to rest in much prettier surroundings.

Emily plopped down onto the ground at the grassy spot where she imagined the foot of Scott's coffin rested. His granite stone gleamed dully in the sunshine, just a small marker that still looked new. Emily breathed in the scent of fresh-mown grass and watched as a few crows glided above the headstones.

"Hey, Mr. Buchanan," Emily said quietly. She and Scott had jokingly referred to each other so formally after a very polite couple who stayed at Eternal Rest one weekend had insisted on addressing them that way. "I know your spirit hasn't crossed over yet, but I also know you're stuck somewhere outside of Oak Hill." Emily waved vaguely. "You got close enough that Kelly sensed you, so that's a good start, and we're doing what we can to try to help you get through."

In between bites of her sandwich, Emily told Scott about the altered photo of Eternal Rest and the reasons it had upset her so much. She liked coming to the cemetery occasionally to unburden her mind to Scott, even though she knew he wasn't actually there—at least, not spiritually—to hear her. Nevertheless, she never wanted to simply unload all her problems and worries, then walk away. She always ended their visits on a positive note.

"July is completely booked. Can you believe it? Every single night of the month! June is close to being booked, too. People are so eager to stay at Eternal Rest that they're willing to move their vacation dates around. They're going for Monday to Wednesday stays, or whatever dates I have free. It feels so good, Scott. I won't be so worried about money, I'll be able to fix the roof, and maybe I'll be able to justify hiring an assistant for more than two days a week. It's been a crazy couple of months, but I'm feeling optimistic."

Emily stood as she crumpled the plastic wrap from her sandwich and stuffed it in the pocket of her jeans. She walked forward, put two fingers against her lips, and leaned down to press them against Scott's headstone. "Bye, Mr. Buchanan. I'll see you soon."

Emily was still stewing over the altered photo of Eternal Rest later that evening, after her shift had ended and she was once again sitting at her rolltop desk. During her first couple of hours at the festival, Emily had been inundated by friends and acquaintances who sought her out to ask her opinion of the piece. She had tried to keep her tone even and her response polite, still reluctant to do or say anything that might reflect badly on the festival or its organizers. By the mid-point of her shift, Emily's canned response had become, "You know that Eternal Rest is a nice place. If the ghosts were scary like that, I wouldn't live there."

Trish had come by Emily's volunteer post at the front entrance, and she said all the things that Emily wanted to but wouldn't. Her tirade about the photo was filled with expletives and vague threats about what she would do to Robert Gaines if she got her hands on him. Emily had actually felt a little better after Trish ran out of steam and left to help an older woman tottering under the weight of a sculpture she had purchased. Trish's venting had helped Emily calm down, and after that, fewer people had been talking about it, so Emily was able to forget about her anger for a while as she lost herself in talking with her fellow volunteers and helping the preview attendees find their way around.

But now, as she sat at home by herself, waiting on her guests to come back from dinner, the anger rose again. Slowly, Emily turned in her chair so she was facing the portrait of her grandparents. They looked so serene there between the front windows, looking out at the results of the hard work they had done to bring Eternal Rest back to life. "Y'all would be appalled at this guy's art of the house," Emily said to them. "Neither one of you ever admitted that this place is haunted, but I'm sure you experienced a lot of the same things I do, so you know the ghosts here are friendly. Grandma, you would have lectured that artist up one side and down the other, if you had been there."

A soft tap sounded behind Emily, and she glanced over her shoulder to see her pencil rolling slowly across the desk. Emily reached out quickly and caught it as it toppled over the edge, then glanced up at the sheet of paper next to her laptop.

What art? Kelly had written.

Emily felt a little startled that Kelly had been writing a message right behind her back. Usually, the ghost waited until no one was in the room with her before spelling out a message. Or, at the very least, she would write in the bedroom while Emily was asleep. The proximity wasn't scary, since Emily trusted Kelly, but it was jarring to think a ghost was hovering so close to her and she couldn't even sense it.

I guess I need to work on that skill.

Now addressing both Kelly and her grandparents— whom Sage said liked to "check in" on Emily and their former home from time to time—Emily launched into a tirade about Robert and his photo of Eternal Rest. Her voice rose as the anger spilled out in the form of words, and she repeated many of the things Trish had said earlier at the festival.

Emily was mid-sentence when she heard a loud bang from the hallway.

9

Emily broke off abruptly and sat up straight, listening. She heard another loud noise and was surprised to realize it was the front door being opened forcefully and then slammed shut. There were several quick footsteps, then Kat strode into the parlor, followed closely by Reed. Emily involuntarily leaned back at the sight of Kat's expression.

"Emily," Kat said with feeling. She walked right up to Emily and put a hand on her shoulder. "We are all just as mad as you about that photograph of your house."

"Everyone is talking about his work," Reed joined in. "He really wants to present Oak Hill in a bad light."

"I appreciate the show of support," Emily said, her body relaxing. Her eyes flicked questioningly to Reed's. His dark eyes didn't give any indication of whether he was there as a friend or something more, though, and Emily had to tell herself, yet again, not to make any teasing comments. Trevor had texted her earlier, suggesting they meet at noon the following day at The Stomping Grounds, a wine and coffee bar just off the square, and she reminded herself that two people could hang out without there being any romantic overtones.

Emily stood and waved toward the sofa and wingback chairs at the front of the room. "Let's go sit. You know, I didn't even see the rest of Robert's work. All I saw was Eternal Rest, and that was enough."

Kat dropped gracefully into one of the chairs. "I am so glad I'm not sleeping under the same roof as him this year."

Reed had disappeared down the hallway instead of sitting, so Emily sat down on the end of the sofa closest to Kat. Eager to change the subject to something more positive, Emily asked, "How was your day?"

Kat's face beamed as she answered, "Outstanding! We got the installation finished up, and I'm so pleased with it. It doesn't officially open until tomorrow, but a few people who were at the cemetery today raved about it. Then, this afternoon, I had quite a few sales. Those early-bird folks come in ready to spend some money."

"I'm glad to hear it. I'm going to the cemetery first thing in the morning to see your installation."

Reed came back into the room then, three wine glasses clinking musically in one hand and a just-opened bottle of cabernet in the other. "I helped myself, Emily. Hope you don't mind."

"Not at all."

As Reed poured the wine and handed the glasses around, the three of them chatted easily, and Emily was relieved that the conversation steered more toward general festival news rather than her own experience.

That feeling only lasted for a short while, when Marianne burst through the front door with a bang and rushed into the parlor as if she were late for an appointment. "You don't have to say it!" Marianne was nearly shouting, and she tugged restlessly at her short salt-and-pepper hair. "Robert Gaines is the devil, and I, for one, told him so!"

Marianne was intense, but Emily reminded herself that at least that intensity was in support of her. She smiled politely and thanked Marianne, torn between wanting to groan at the reintroduction of the subject and wanting to laugh at Marianne's indignance on her behalf.

Emily was glad when Marianne declined the offer of a glass of wine, saying that she needed a shower and bed. As she retreated upstairs, Greg Van Breda came in, making almost no noise as he shyly appeared in the parlor doorway.

"Hello, Greg," Emily said. She realized her voice had a singsong tone to it, the voice she might use if she were speaking to a scared child. "Did you have a nice day at the festival?"

Greg nodded slightly. "It was a very good day," he answered. He blinked at Emily a few times before adding, "Your B and B is a nice place, and everyone knows it." He gave a short nod, as if that statement was all that needed to be said on the subject, and disappeared from the doorway.

Emily snickered when she caught Reed's startled expression. "That's Greg, a sculptor," she explained. "He's a man of few words."

"But the words he said were good ones," Kat said, waving her wine glass in the direction of the spot Greg had just occupied with his broad body. "One mean artist won't hurt your reputation."

"Kat is right," Reed joined in. "In fact, that photo might even be good for your business. Just look at how busy you've been since Eternal Rest has been involved in two other scandals."

"Thanks, you two. I appreciate the optimism. I wish there was some way I could get that photo taken down, but it's like the situation with the other places around Oak Hill. He took photos of public buildings and businesses, and there's no law to say you can't do that."

Kat raised her eyebrows conspiratorially. "Who says you have to obey the law?"

As soon as Gretchen arrived the next morning, Emily went upstairs to neaten the guest rooms as quickly as she could. She was anxious to walk next door to the cemetery to see Kat's art, but she knew it was wise to get her tasks done beforehand.

It was mid-morning by the time Emily made the short walk along the path that led from Eternal Rest to the ornate iron gate of Hilltop Cemetery. As she began moving up the brick path that led straight from the gate to the top of the hill, she didn't immediately spot any kind of art.

When Emily reached the intersection with the fourth path that ringed the hill, she glanced to her right and spotted Reed and his team a short distance away. Emily walked up to them, said good morning, and was about to ask where the art was when she noticed a tall man in a charcoal-gray suit out of the corner of her eye. "Oh! Who's over there at your family's plot, Reed?"

Even as she was speaking, Emily realized she wasn't looking at a man at all. It was a life-size painting of an elderly African-American man who was gazing serenely at the Marshall family's ancestral plot. Instead of being painted onto canvas, though, the work had been done on a thick, clear piece of acrylic that had been placed in a stand. Emily gasped and put a hand on Reed's arm. "It's your great-great-grandfather, isn't it?"

Reed smiled proudly. "Paul Artemis Marshall. Kat used the only portrait ever painted of him for reference."

"It's incredible." Even that praise felt like an understatement.

"He's not alone. There are five more people depicted around Hilltop. Kat chose six notable Oak Hill residents who are buried here. I've been working with her for months on this project, helping her choose the right people and trying to track down old pictures or portraits of them. I wanted to tell you so badly, because I knew you'd love it, but I also knew it would be better as a surprise."

"Where's Kat?"

"I think she's over by Walt Archer."

Emily admired the painting of Reed's great-great-grandfather for a while longer before making her way toward the Archer mausoleum. It was situated at the very top of the hill on which Hilltop Cemetery was built, an appropriate place for Oak Hill's first mayor. As Emily walked up, Kat was just finishing arranging a few flower-pots filled with daisies around the base of the painting.

Kat turned when she heard Emily approaching. "The flowers hide the base, so it looks more like a real person standing here when you just glance at it," Kat explained.

Walt Archer had been a short man, and Emily recognized his round face and balding head from the portrait of him that hung in the atrium at Oak Hill City Hall. "I love it," Emily enthused. "You've brought my cemetery to life in a way I never imagined, and I can't wait for people to see it this week."

Kat nodded toward a spot somewhere behind Emily. "And here they come."

Emily turned and saw a group of about twenty people heading up the walkway. She had never seen such a large group at Hilltop before. Her eyes moved to the grassy parking area along the road, and she saw a small bus parked there. "Is someone giving tours?"

"Yeah, the festival has a shuttle that will take people to the remote installations around town. Didn't they tell you?"

Emily looked at Kat sheepishly. "I'm sure it was sent out in an email. I haven't been doing a good job keeping up with news the city sends out, even when it involves my house or Hilltop. I'm going to look at the rest of the paintings, so enjoy greeting your adoring fans!"

Kat actually looked a little nervous at that suggestion, and she eyed the approaching tour group with trepidation. Emily just smiled reassuringly and walked down the side of the hill that faced away from Eternal Rest.

By the time she had admired the rest of Kat's paintings, another busload of art lovers had shown up, and the parking lot was full of cars. The cemetery had been flooded with visitors when Kelly Stern's body had been discovered there, and this time, Emily enjoyed seeing people flocking to Hilltop for a reason that was so much more positive. When Emily went back to the house for her purse, she found Gretchen speaking in a friendly tone to someone clearly calling to book two rooms, which only added to Emily's feeling of satisfaction.

As Emily drove into downtown Oak Hill to meet Trevor, she felt better than she had in recent weeks. Even though Scott's situation still weighed heavily on her mind, not to mention Robert Gaines's interpretation of Eternal Rest, there was an optimism Emily hadn't sensed in a long time. It felt like good things were happening, and she was looking forward to the first official day of the festival and the energy of the crowd.

Emily parked in the volunteer lot at the high school again, then walked to The Stomping Grounds. Like many businesses in the area of the square, the wine and coffee bar was in an old house that had been converted into a business. The downstairs of the white clapboard structure housed the cafe, and the upstairs had two rooms that could be rented out for private parties and meetings. Emily went inside, but Trevor wasn't among the few people seated around the tables or settled into overstuffed chairs nestled in the corners of the room. Emily walked out onto the front porch, intending to grab an empty table out there since the day was so nice, but before she could sit, she saw Trevor hurrying along the sidewalk from the direction of the square. Something about the stiffness of his body and his hurried gait instantly told Emily that something was wrong. All the optimism she had felt on the drive over disappeared.

Trevor stopped at the bottom of the porch stairs as Emily took a few steps down. He looked up at her anxiously, his chest heaving. "One of the artists just died right in the middle of his booth. Robert Gaines is dead."

Emily froze on the bottom step of the porch and stared at Trevor as her mind tried to process what he had just said. For a brief moment, her mind seemed to go entirely blank. Then, just as quickly, it was replaced by a flood of thoughts all competing for dominance. One of them rose above the others. *Someone killed Robert Gaines because that photo made Eternal Rest look so dark and scary.*

No, Emily quickly told herself, that was a ridiculous idea. The thought that someone would commit murder on Emily's behalf was not only far-fetched, but also chilling. However, the idea that someone would kill because they were so offended at the way Robert had made them, their business, or their town look wasn't such a stretch. The memory of Jess sitting on the grass in the square, surrounded by angry, sympathetic volunteers, flashed into her mind. Reed's words the night before, about how everyone was talking about the unkind way Robert Gaines had portrayed Oak Hill, quickly followed.

"They think he had a heart attack," Trevor said, snapping Emily out of her suspicious train of thinking.

Emily blinked. "What?"

"Robert, the artist. Apparently, he was taking a quick lunch break, so he had pulled the front flap of his tent closed. The artist across the row from him noticed the tent had been closed for a long time, so they went to check on him, and they found him just lying on the ground in the middle of his booth. They think maybe he had a heart attack."

"When did this happen?"

"Just now. I was walking down that row to come here, right after the other artist found his body. People were shouting, and a crowd was starting to gather, and someone was yelling about calling an ambulance for a man who'd had a heart attack." Trevor frowned. "He looked perfectly healthy when I spoke to him yesterday, but of course, just because you look good on the outside, doesn't mean you look good on the inside."

Emily suppressed a wry smile at Trevor's apt statement. Even though he was talking about Robert's health, she felt like it also applied to him in a broader sense. He looked like any other artist, yet there he was, upsetting everyone with his dark, twisted vision of their little town.

And now he was dead.

With a longing glance over her shoulder toward the empty table on the porch, Emily stood up straight, hitched her purse strap higher on her shoulder, and said, "Right. Let's go, then. I'm guessing the festival will need all hands on deck."

As they walked briskly toward the square, Trevor glanced at Emily. "I guess we'll have to reschedule."

"Dead bodies really get in the way of my social life," Emily answered. She had meant to say it sarcastically, jokingly even, but it was all too true. *At least, this time, it's just a death and not a murder.*

There were two police cars and one ambulance parked along one of the streets that lined the square. Emily thought it was funny that the police would bother to drive over, when the Oak Hill Police Department was just one block away. There were clusters of people on the sidewalk, all gesturing toward the rows of tents and talking rapidly to each other.

Trevor and Emily worked their way along the edge of the crowd until they reached an entrance to the square. Inside, all shopping had ceased. There were groups of people clogging the aisles between tents, shaking their heads grimly, but also individuals and families who were gazing around uncertainly, as if they wanted to continue looking at art but weren't sure it was the polite thing to do at such a time.

The row that included Robert Gaines's booth had already been cordoned off by the police, who had not only strung yellow tape across each end, but also positioned officers along it to tell people to stay back.

Emily and Trevor were making their way toward the volunteer tent to find out what they could do to help when Emily glanced over and saw that Roger Newton was one of the officers guarding the closed row. She told Trevor she would meet him shortly, then pushed her way past a few people who were watching the proceedings, their expressions a mix of horror and fascination.

Roger saw Emily as she popped out from between two tall men and closed the gap between herself and the yellow tape. He smiled grimly at her and said, "At least this time, Miss Emily, it doesn't have anything to do with you or your ghosts."

"Do they know what happened?"

Roger kept his voice low, but his tone had a slight reprimanding edge to it. "Nothing scandalous. Looks like a heart attack or a stroke, maybe. Bad timing to die right in the middle of the arts festival, but it was just his time to go."

Emily nodded and thanked Roger before turning and plunging into the crowd again. When she reached the volunteer tent, all she could see was a wall of lime-green shirts. She finally identified Trevor by his dark hair, which was sticking up at increasingly wild angles as he nervously ran his hands through it. As she got closer to him, Emily recognized another head of hair, too: Sage's pink spikes. Sage broke off whatever she was saying to Trevor when she saw Emily. "There you are! I closed my booth and came over here when I found out what was happening. You think someone killed him to get revenge for Eternal Rest?"

"Sage!" Emily cried. She lowered her voice as she added, "You can't say something like that! What if the police think I... you know."

"Oh, we know you didn't kill anyone." Sage, unlike Emily, wasn't bothering to speak in quieter tones, and Emily could see a few astonished glances out of the corner of her eye. "It is odd, though, that of all the artists to wind up dead, it's the one so many people are mad at."

Emily and Trevor had to agree with that, but Emily relayed what Roger had told her, adding, "So, it looks like he just died of natural causes, though I can certainly see why people might be suspicious."

This time, when Sage spoke again, she did use a lower voice. She was so quiet that Emily and Trevor had to lean in to hear her, their three heads nearly touching. "I hope that's the case, because Jen and the rest of the festival team are going to have a tough enough time as it is. Just having a death at the event is going to be a PR nightmare." Sage threw a look over Emily's shoulder, then spoke even more softly. "Still, I think his death was intentional."

Emily knew Sage well enough to trust her instincts on things like this, but Trevor frowned at her. "The police don't think so."

"I know, but I hope they investigate thoroughly. I knew someone had died before I ever heard people start shouting about it. I felt it, like a presence that just popped up in my mind. I could feel its confusion, but I also felt its sense of betrayal."

Emily chewed nervously on a fingernail as she thought. "Maybe he felt betrayed by his heart for not working the way it was supposed to."

Sage just gave Emily a flat look, as if to say, *Seriously?*

"Okay, probably not," Emily conceded. "Maybe you are right, Sage, but I've had enough murder to last me a lifetime. It's a shame someone died, but I'm happy to let it be just a regular old death."

Sage glanced at Trevor. "Remember this conversation when I get to say 'I told you so' later on."

"Can't you just ask the guy's ghost what happened?" Trevor asked.

"Only if it's still around." Sage spread her hands. "I felt him in that moment of death, but that doesn't mean his spirit is going to stay on this plane. I don't feel him now, so he could have crossed over, or he could have wandered off somewhere. Maybe he's watching over his body, or keeping an eye on his killer."

Sage's voice had started to rise in volume again, and at that last word, Emily saw more startled glances from the volunteers around them. She was relieved when she heard a woman's shout and the wave of shushing that rolled through the group. Jen must have climbed up on a chair, because her head and shoulders were floating above the lime-green sea. "Volunteers!" she shouted as everyone gathered closer to her. Sage remained, too, and Emily guessed she was there partly from curiosity, but also to support her wife through what had to be a strange, stressful situation.

Jen was still standing on the chair, but now she was able

to dial back the volume of her voice as everyone quieted down. "The best thing we can do right now is get things back up and running. You know, back to normal. The police are taking Robert to the ambulance right now, and then that row will reopen to the public. If anyone asks you about it, let them know that he died of natural causes, but don't say anything more than that. And please, if attendees don't ask about it, then don't bring it up. Remember, we're going for normal. We want people to have fun, buy art, and then come back next year to do it all over again. Thank you!"

As Jen jumped off the chair, Emily turned to Trevor and Sage. "I'm off to the help station, then," Emily said. "Time to give directions to the tourists."

"And I'm reopening my booth. Something tells me that if everyone has death on the brain, it might be good for my business." At first, Emily thought Sage was joking, but one look showed that her friend was absolutely serious. Emily felt slightly horrified by the idea, until she realized Sage was right. She might even make a few dollars off people who wanted to talk to the ghost of Robert Gaines himself.

Trevor said he was going to help deliver bottles of water to the artists, and the three of them all parted, promising to catch up soon.

The afternoon sped past for Emily. She gave the "natural causes" answer to dozens of inquiring people, and the repetition helped the shock of what had happened wear off. She tried to analyze her feelings in between giving directions to the beer tent and telling a sweaty, red-faced woman that, no, there was nowhere at an outdoor festival that had air-conditioning. Despite her hurt feelings over his depiction of Eternal Rest, Emily actually felt sad that Robert Gaines had died. She wondered what it had been like for him, dying alone inside his little tent, while thousands of people who could have helped were passing by outside, completely oblivious. It wasn't a nice way to go, for anyone. When he had stayed at Eternal Rest, Robert had always struck Emily as arrogant but not malicious. He wasn't mean and vindictive like Jaxon Knight-MacGinn had been, so it was easier to feel sorry about his demise.

The crowds had thinned out significantly by the final hour of the festival, and eventually, one of the other volunteers tapped Emily on the shoulder. "You can head out early, if you want," she told Emily. "I think we can handle the few stragglers."

As she accepted the offer and said her thanks, Emily realized how grateful she really was to be done for the day. She felt exhausted. Despite the fact that none of the events of the day had to do with her, Robert was still someone she had known. Even if he had been a stranger to her, the fact remained that someone had died at the festival, and all the questions and speculation had just drained her energy.

Emily decided to stop by Sage's booth to see how business was going, but first, her curiosity got the better of her, and she turned down the row where Robert's booth was. She had expected to see the tent closed up so no one could go inside. Instead, it was wide open, all of his artwork still on display.

As Emily walked closer, she saw someone handing a stack of cash to a man in khaki slacks and a white button-down shirt. She heard the man say, "Thank you so much for your support. His widow will need every penny she can get."

A lawyer, maybe. But hadn't Marianne said that Robert was getting divorced? Was his wife swooping in to make money just hours after his death?

No sooner had the first customer walked away than another one stepped forward, credit card in hand. Emily looked into Robert's booth and saw how many blank spots there were. Now that he was dead, everyone wanted to buy his work. She didn't know if people thought it would be more valuable, or if they wanted a grim souvenir of the time they went to an arts festival and somebody died.

As Emily's eyes continued to rove across the artwork, she realized the altered photo of Eternal Rest was gone.

That night, Emily sat in the parlor with a book and a glass of wine, though her mind wasn't really processing the words her eyes were taking in. There were too many thoughts whirling inside her head, ranging from whether Sage's speculations were correct to who in their right mind could have possibly looked at the photo of Eternal Rest and felt compelled to buy it.

As her guests began to return, each one came into the parlor to speak with Emily for a few minutes. All any of them could talk about, of course, was Robert Gaines, with the exception of Greg. He came in, asked Emily quietly if she was doing all right, then turned and left before Emily could return the question.

Marianne's voice was as loud as ever, and Emily decided it was more grating after a very long day than first thing in the morning. "What a crazy day!" Marianne had a takeout bag in one hand, and she raised her arm toward Emily. "Mind if I stick this in the fridge? The cake at The Depot looked so good I couldn't pass it up, but I was too full to eat it by the time they cut me a slice. How about Robert? What a day. My sales weren't good at all today. People were too busy gossiping to actually look at my work. How about you? Did you have your hands full as a volunteer?"

Emily actually had to pause for a moment before answering Marianne, just to give herself time to process such a long stream of information. "We managed," Emily eventually answered. "I'm sorry your sales were down. Hopefully, you'll make up for it tomorrow."

"Let's hope. The weather should be perfect tomorrow, and comfortable people are more likely to spend money than sweaty people. Good night!"

Emily was still trying to recover from the vocal onslaught when Kat returned. Tonight, there was no Reed in tow. "How was your day?" Emily asked her. She had never seen Kat looking so exhausted, and Emily noticed that some of her eyeliner was streaked, as if she had been rubbing her eyes.

Kat's eyes widened in shock. "Didn't you hear? One of the artists died today!"

"Oh, believe me, I know," Emily said. "I guess I should have asked how your day was, despite the fact that someone died at the festival."

"Overwhelming, actually. It was a good day for me financially, but I'm wiped out."

Kat was just heading up the stairs as Jake and Selena returned. They reported that their afternoon had been steady. Emily had the silly thought that her guests were like the Goldilocks of the festival: Marianne's sales had been too low, Kat's had been too high, but Jake and Selena's had been just right.

The idea and the ridiculous image it conjured in Emily's imagination were her cue to go to bed. She followed Jake and Selena out of the parlor, wishing them a good night as they went upstairs and Emily walked to the back of the hallway. She popped into the kitchen to prep the coffee maker for the next morning, then walked across the hall to her bedroom. All of the thoughts that had made her feel wakeful before were finally quieted, and Emily was asleep in minutes.

On Friday morning, Emily could sense there was a more relaxed atmosphere at breakfast as she grabbed the empty butter dish from the sideboard and took it back to the kitchen to refill it. Even though the artists were talking with each other over their coffee and Grainy Day baked goods about how excited they were for the day ahead, they were clearly in less of a hurry to get to the square. Their booths were already set up, so there was no point in being there early.

Jake and Selena were the last to leave, and by the time they headed out the door, Gretchen had already arrived. Her eyes had been wide when she came in, but she waited until it was just her and Emily in the house before engaging in anything other than light small talk.

Emily was in the kitchen, loading breakfast plates into the dishwasher, when Gretchen appeared in the doorway, bouncing anxiously on the balls of her feet. "Did you see the body?"

"No, it happened before I got there. And I know you like true crime, but a friend of mine who's a police officer said it looked like a heart attack. I guess being an artist is more stressful than any of us realized."

"Oh." Gretchen actually looked disappointed. The phone started ringing, and she took off down the hall to answer it. A moment later, she reappeared in the kitchen doorway, her excitement back in full force. She handed the cordless phone to Emily as she whispered, "It's a Detective Hernandez from the Oak Hill Police Department."

Emily frowned slightly as she took the phone and lifted it to her ear. "Good morning, this is Emily."

"Good morning, Emily. It's Danny Hernandez calling."

A little laugh escaped Emily's lips before she could stop herself. "I hate to admit it, but I've been thinking of Detective as your first name. Your business card only has your first initial on it."

Danny sighed dramatically. "You're not the first to say that. The next time I get business cards printed, I'm going to put my full name on there: Detective Daniel Andres Hernandez. You can call me whichever of those names you like best."

Emily smiled into the phone. "What can I do for you this morning, *Detective*?"

Danny's voice turned serious. "I'm calling about Robert Gaines. I understand he sold a photo of your B and B yesterday. Were you two friends?"

"No. He's a former guest, though. He stayed here last year. And just to be clear, I didn't know he was using Eternal Rest in his art until I saw the piece myself. I hope whoever bought it has already burned it."

"I didn't see it. Was it not good?"

"He made my home look like something from a horror movie."

"Hmm. He definitely seemed determined to, ah, show Oak Hill in a different light."

"So I've heard."

"Did you speak to him about the art of your house?"

"Briefly. He was very proud of it."

Danny cleared his throat. "I realize it sounds like I'm questioning you. Rest assured, you're not a suspect."

Emily had been idly wiping down the countertop while she and Danny spoke, but her hand froze. "Suspect? I thought Robert died of a heart attack."

"That can't be confirmed at this time."

"Oh."

"Which is why I'm calling you."

"Oh?"

"I realize you had a vested interest in the Knight-MacGinn case, since he was your guest and you found the body." Danny hesitated, then quickly said, "I thought you and Sage Clark might want to come lend a hand again."

"Oh!"

"It would be unofficial help, of course. Engaging psychics and trying to glean information from ghosts isn't exactly the way we conduct police business here, but I thought maybe you two could help point our investigation in the right direction."

Emily nearly said "oh" again, then realized she really needed to give Danny something more to work with. "Well," she said thoughtfully, "I'm definitely willing to help out however possible, but it's Sage who's the psychic medium, not me."

"I called Sage already. She's agreed to help but insists your growing skills will be an asset, too."

Emily shook her head as a corner of her mouth lifted. "Of course she did. Count me in."

"Great. Can you be at the station at eleven?"

"I'll see you then."

Emily hung up the phone, feeling both pleased and perplexed. Being asked by a detective to help with a case was a strange feeling, and it was even more strange to think that the case was the death of Robert Gaines, which everyone had been told was completely natural. Even though Emily's mind had gone right to murder when Trevor had first told her the news yesterday, one of the reasons she had dismissed it was because it happened right in the middle of the festival. Who went around killing when there were so many people present? It seemed like the risk of getting caught would be too high.

Maybe it wasn't planned. Maybe Robert was in an argument with someone, and they killed him without even thinking about it.

With those kinds of thoughts whirling through her mind, Emily went into the parlor, where she knew Gretchen would be anxiously waiting to find out why an Oak Hill Police Department Detective had called Emily the day after a death.

Emily made Gretchen promise not to tell anyone what Danny had relayed, so of course Emily knew that by lunchtime, everyone in town would have heard about it.

Sage was already waiting as Emily walked up to the front door of the Oak Hill Police Department. Reaching the historic brick building had taken a while, since the streets around downtown Oak Hill had gotten more and more busy the closer Emily got to the festival. The police department was located a block away from the square, and while the drive from Eternal Rest into downtown normally took just ten minutes, today it took twenty. After Emily had parked in the volunteer lot at the school, figuring she would just head to the festival after the meeting with Hernandez, she had to fight a different kind of traffic on the sidewalks, as a crowd of eager art lovers made their way to the square.

Instead of saying hello, Sage dove in with, "How is it that every year, I forget how bad traffic is during the festival? It was already backed up when I came in to set up my booth this morning!"

"Who's watching your booth, anyway?"

Sage smiled wickedly. "Jen found a volunteer who was willing to keep an eye on things. She's telling anyone who stops by that I'm helping with a police investigation and will be back after lunch. I might miss out on a little money this morning, but it's great publicity for me. A lot of skeptics are more likely to give me a try if they know that even the police believe in me."

"Clever move. Also, nice move on making me be a part of this. I suppose this is yet another exercise to help me develop my skills?"

"Of course! How's it been going with the Tarot card exercise?"

Emily grimaced. "Kind of non-existent. I had one sort of weird experience with them, which I'll tell you about later, but otherwise, it's been a little too hectic for me to really give them a proper trial."

"Yeah, I realize this week might not be good timing." Sage opened the door and held it for Emily as she continued, "But, you have them in your possession now, and you're thinking about them, so when you finally have some quiet time next week, you'll be better prepared mentally."

As Sage and Emily arrived at the front desk, Danny Hernandez was just coming out to find them. "Right on time," he said. His smile reminded Emily of some gossip Sage had recently shared with her, and she could easily see why ladies in Oak Hill were taken with Danny's easy smile, brown eyes, and dark, wavy hair. He seemed to realize Emily was staring at him because he reached up to smooth his black polo shirt.

Emily blinked and returned Danny's smile. "Good morning again, Detective Hernandez."

"Sage, Emily. Thanks for coming on such short notice. Follow me." Danny turned and led the way to his office. After he ushered the two women inside, he shut the door before moving to sit behind his desk. "Please, sit."

Emily hadn't even settled into her chair before Danny began to speak. "You both know why I called you in, but the situation is more serious than I implied on the phone. Sage, I think you saw right through my vague hints."

Sage turned and winked at Emily. "I'm about to have my chance to say, 'I told you so.'"

Danny raised an eyebrow at Sage's comment, but he continued. "It's not that we simply suspect Robert Gaines didn't die of natural causes. We actually have good evidence that he was murdered."

Emily slid to the edge of her seat and leaned forward, propping her elbows on Danny's desk. "But how? Roger told me it looked like a heart attack. Besides, who would murder someone in the middle of the festival?"

Danny shook his head grimly. "I can't answer either of those questions yet. The coroner found what appear to be chemical burns in Robert's mouth and throat, so we've ordered a full autopsy. It looks as though he ingested something toxic. What that substance was, or how it wound up inside Robert Gaines, is still a complete mystery."

12

Emily flopped back in her chair and turned her face to the ceiling, her eyes shut tight.

"Em?" Sage managed to inject a lot of concern into that one word.

With a soft groan, Emily brought her hands to her face and massaged her forehead. "I'm so done with murders."

Danny sounded hesitant as he said, "I thought you agreed to come meet me today because you also think Gaines's death wasn't natural, and you wanted to help."

Emily sat up and looked at Danny. "You're right. It's not that I'm surprised, so much as I'm just tired of people being murdered."

"Oh, it's not that bad," Sage said. "You've only had two murders recently: Jaxon and now Robert. Kelly and the three hotel owners were all old murders that happened when you were a lot younger."

Emily rolled her eyes. "That doesn't make me feel better."

Sage's tone turned businesslike as she directed her attention toward Danny again. "I expect you want us to try to make contact with the artist's ghost. Would you like us to hold a séance at his booth?"

Danny shook his head. "I don't think that's something I can formally facilitate. Your booth isn't so far from his, though. Do you think you could try to contact him from there?"

The corners of Sage's mouth tightened. "I'll try, but I can't guarantee it will get me anywhere. Like I told you on the phone, Detective, I felt Robert's presence at the moment of his death, but I haven't sensed it since then. I've even reached out psychically to look for him, but I've gotten nothing. It's possible there's no ghost for us to communicate with. If Robert's spirit has moved on, then he won't be telling us what happened."

"I understand, and I appreciate your willingness to give this a try. In the meantime, ladies, I don't think there's much more we can do right now. Just keep me posted on any contact that you make, please."

Emily and Sage assured Danny they would pass along any paranormal gossip they heard, shook hands with him, and left. Neither of the women spoke until they were on the sidewalk in front of the police station, where the clear sky and warm sun promised a pleasant afternoon for the arts festival.

"I'm not sure I'll be any help with this," Emily finally said.

"You won't be with that attitude! This is good practice for you, Em. I think it might help your development pick up pace." As she spoke, Sage pulled a pair of sunglasses out of her purse and put them on. Their bright-yellow frames made it hard to take her advice seriously, but Emily nodded dutifully. She knew arguing with Sage about this was no use. In fact, Emily wasn't at all against the idea of helping Sage contact a ghost, though "helping" didn't seem like the right word. Sitting next to Sage and providing moral support was about all Emily could offer, but it would still be an interesting experience for her. Emily's reluctance was simply because she wasn't looking forward to being involved in yet another murder investigation.

After this, I'm taking a vacation. Even if I can't go anywhere, I'm at least taking a break from dead bodies.

As if to punctuate her thought, Emily's stomach suddenly gave a loud growl. She sucked in her breath in surprise as she clamped a hand over her belly. "Sorry! I guess I didn't eat enough breakfast!"

Sage just laughed. "Good thing I was just about to suggest we grab a quick lunch at The Depot. You've got some time before your volunteer shift, right?"

Emily checked her watch and realized she still had plenty of time. Their meeting with Hernandez had been brief.

The Depot wasn't crowded yet since it was still a little early for lunch, and Sage and Emily were soon seated at one of the tables set up on the patio in front of the restaurant. Just a few minutes after putting in their orders, Emily's cell phone rang. She picked her phone up, saw Trevor's name on the caller ID, and put it down. She was surprised Trevor would be calling her, but not wanting to be rude to her lunch companion, she told Sage, "I'll call him back after we eat."

"No, take it. It's important."

"It is?"

"Yes, now answer before it goes to voicemail!" Sage looked torn between amusement and exasperation.

When Emily answered the phone, there was a long silence, and she thought for a moment that she had, in fact, waited too long. She was just about to say hello again when she heard Trevor's quiet voice. Emily had to press her phone hard against one ear while she plugged the other with a finger. It sounded like Trevor was trying to avoid being overheard by anyone around him.

"Emily, um, something weird is going on."

Emily sat up straight, instantly concerned. "Are you okay?"

"I'm fine. It's... ghost stuff."

Ghost stuff? "Tell me what's happening."

"It will be easier to show you once you're here. Can you come to the festival early today?"

"Sure. Sage and I are at The Depot right now. We just ordered, so we can come over after we eat. Whatever it is, I'm sure Sage will want to know about it, too."

"She will," Trevor agreed, "and I can actually bring what I have to show you to the restaurant." He refused to give any more details, but he promised to be there within twenty minutes. In the meantime, Sage and Emily could only speculate what Trevor had meant by saying that instead of telling them his story, he had to show them. When their lunch arrived, both of them only picked at their food as they continued to consider the possibilities.

Emily had only eaten a few bites of her club sandwich by the time Trevor arrived. He dragged an empty chair from a nearby table and squeezed in between Emily and Sage. He took his sunglasses off, his blue eyes looking intently at both women. "You're not going to believe this," he said, skipping right over a greeting.

"Oh, I think we will," Sage said, smiling.

"I've been taking a ton of pictures with my phone," Trevor began. "Since I'm working during both the morning and afternoon shifts, I've offered to take pictures of volunteers doing their thing. Later, we'll put them online with a thank you message, that sort of thing. Anyway, this morning I wound up taking pictures that had Robert Gaines's booth in the shots. I didn't think anything of it at the time, because I just noticed volunteers talking to attendees and started snapping. But later—" Trevor broke off as a server came over just then, and he hastily ordered a sandwich before looking at Sage and Emily apologetically.

"Sorry, but I'm starving, so I may as well eat while I'm here."

Trevor paused again as he gathered his thoughts, and Emily realized she had a French fry gripped tightly between two fingers. She wasn't even sure when she had picked it up, but she was so engrossed in Trevor's story she had forgotten to eat it. Now, she dropped it back onto her plate and wiped her fingers on her napkin as she waited anxiously for Trevor to continue.

"I had a short break, so I went to the volunteer tent so I could sit in the shade for a little while," Trevor said, picking back up. "I started scrolling through the pictures, and I saw the weirdest thing in one of them. First, I noticed there was someone in the picture who seemed transparent: you can see through their body to the booth they're standing in front of, which happens to be Robert's. Then, when I zoomed in, I realized it looks just like Robert Gaines. Check it out."

Trevor pulled out his cell phone, selected the photo in question, and presented it to Emily. She raised the phone close to her face to peer at the screen. It was difficult to see in the sunshine, but she could make out the figure Trevor was pointing to. "I can kind of see what you're talking about," she said slowly, "but I'm sure it would be easier to see in a darker place, like the tent. Also, I'd like to see it on a bigger screen."

"I can email it to you two."

"Perfect," Sage said as she reached out for the phone to have her own look. She took off her sunglasses and squinted at the screen for a long time before finally saying, "You can definitely see through this person. I don't know what Robert looked like, so I can't say whether there's a resemblance, but I know Emily can confirm that for you."

"I'm confused," Emily broke in. "Sage, you said that you couldn't sense Robert's presence anymore, that he seemed to only be around immediately after he died. If this photo really shows his ghost, then how come you can't sense him?"

"That's a good question. Maybe it's something like the situation with Jaxon Knight-MacGinn, and his ghost isn't there at the festival all the time. It's possible that Robert's ghost and I haven't been in the same place at the same time since his death."

The server returned and plunked a huge glass of sweet tea onto the table in front of Trevor. He took a long drink, then said, "I can't believe I took a photo of a ghost."

"Without even trying to, no less," Emily said. "You know, I have a lot of guests who try to do this all the time, and here you did it like it was nothing!"

Sage smiled proudly at Trevor. "You did a great job! Not just in taking the photo, but in looking close enough to realize there was a ghost in it. Most people wouldn't have caught that kind of detail, since at a glance, he's just another person in the background."

Trevor gave a little shrug, but he was smiling, too. "I think it's the way the ghost seemed to be looking right at me in the photo. It was hard to miss."

Sage began telling Trevor about how she and Emily were hoping to assist the police. Trevor was shocked to hear it was murder rather than a simple heart attack, but he offered to help however he could. "If you need an extra hand in a séance, count me in. This time, at least, I don't have to worry about the killer being anyone in my family."

"How is your dad doing, anyway?" Sage asked. Emily could feel the warmth in her cheeks as she blushed, but she knew Sage didn't feel any embarrassment about asking Trevor such a pointed question.

Apparently, Trevor didn't feel any embarrassment about it, either. His tone was light as he answered, "He's hanging in there. Being in jail might actually be good for him, as far as his health is concerned. He's less likely to overexert himself there than he was at home."

Emily had been amazed when Trevor had told her that he visited his father in jail, since not only had Benjamin Williams killed Kelly Stern, but he had also tried to kill Trevor and his brother. Still, Emily knew that Benjamin's time was running out, since his chemo treatments could only extend his life, not save it. She admired Trevor for wanting to show his father some love and forgiveness while he still could. If Emily was in Trevor's situation, she didn't know if she could be as big-hearted about it.

Trevor's food arrived soon, and Emily finally gave her own meal the attention it deserved. She had just taken a huge bite of sandwich when a shadow fell over her. She craned her head around and saw Jay, the owner of The Depot, looming over their table. Emily gave a little wave as she tried to chew and swallow quickly so she could give him a proper greeting.

"I hear that artist was murdered," Jay said, leaning over their table so he wouldn't be overheard. He nodded toward Sage and winked. "You'll have to tell us if his ghost shows up to reveal the name of his killer!"

Everyone at the table burst out laughing. Finally, Sage beamed up at Jay and promised, "You'll be the second person I tell, right after Detective Hernandez!"

Emily felt reluctant to leave The Depot. After looking at Trevor's possibly paranormal photo, she had enjoyed having his and Sage's company as they finished eating. Trevor and Sage had become friends in high school, and even though they had only reconnected recently, when Trevor moved back to Oak Hill to take care of his dad, they still had an easy rapport with each other. Emily had been content to listen to Trevor and Sage reminisce about former classmates as she idly dabbed her dwindling fries in ketchup.

"You heard that Elena Ford joined a circus, right?" Sage was saying. "A real, honest-to-goodness circus! Whenever my dad gives me grief about making a living as a psychic medium, I remind him that I could have joined the circus instead. Of course, I think he might have preferred that."

As one o'clock approached, the three of them walked to the festival together. Sage was eager to get her booth opened up for the afternoon, though she also hoped for enough downtime that she could send out mental feelers for Robert's ghost. Trevor and Emily said goodbye to her as she turned down the row her booth was on, then continued on their way to the volunteer tent.

"Where will you be stationed today?" Trevor asked.

"Wherever they need me. I'm happy to do anything as long as it has nothing to do with Robert Gaines."

Trevor gave Emily a sidelong glance. "I would apologize for bringing the picture to your attention, but since you're already working with the police…"

Emily turned to Trevor as she slowed her pace. "Don't feel bad for showing us! I'm glad you brought it to our attention, and it might be especially helpful for Sage. I'm just hoping for an ordinary afternoon. This festival is one of the few times I get to escape Eternal Rest, so I don't want anybody keeling over and getting in the way of my enjoyment."

Even though she couldn't see his eyes behind his sunglasses, Emily knew Trevor was looking at her keenly. "Is that really how you think of it? That you're trapped at Eternal Rest and have to escape?"

Emily's pace slowed even more, and finally she came to a stop. Trevor turned so he could face Emily fully, taking off his sunglasses as he did. Emily stared down at the grass, which was already turning brown after being trampled on by so many festival visitors. "Maybe, sometimes." She felt guilty saying the words, as if she were betraying her life's work and, maybe, her grandparents, too. "I love owning a bed and breakfast, and I love that house and all the memories there, but it's hard without Scott. I really need someone to help me full-time, but I need to make more money before that can happen. Until then, I'm stuck there most of the time."

"Scott was your husband, right?"

Emily nodded despondently as she realized she also felt like she was betraying Scott. It wasn't his fault he had died, and she didn't ever want to sound like she was complaining about the fact that he was no longer around to help run Eternal Rest.

Trevor turned and began walking again, one hand on

Emily's arm to gently coax her into motion. His tone was gentle as he said, "It's hard when we're settled into our routine with someone and rely on them for things, and then suddenly they aren't there one day. It's difficult to balance grieving their absence and allowing yourself to be a little angry about the situation it puts you in."

Emily glanced up at Trevor. The corners of his mouth were turned down, and she knew he was referring to his own experience with his brother's sudden disappearance. Trevor had only been fifteen years old at the time, and she knew he had looked up to Dillan.

"Was it hard living with your dad after Dillan left?"

"He had always been strict with us, but he was so angry after Dillan left town, and it just got worse. I couldn't do anything right in his eyes, and it got to the point where I pretty much hid in my room whenever I was home so I wouldn't have to risk seeing him. I moved out the day after I graduated high school. Dad got better as time went on, and when I got older, I could finally enjoy coming home for Christmas and Thanksgiving. Still, Dillan's name was like a swear word in our house. If anyone mentioned him, Dad would get angry all over again, like he did back when Dillan first disappeared."

Emily knew Trevor loved his brother, but she could understand why he would feel some resentment about Dillan leaving Oak Hill. He had felt abandoned.

With a sensation like an invisible knife was stabbing her heart, Emily realized she felt resentment toward Scott, too. He hadn't meant to leave her all alone, but there was still that part of her that felt hurt by his death.

Even two years after Scott's car crash, Emily could still be surprised by the strange feelings her grief brought to the surface.

Trevor was silent, either too absorbed in his own thoughts to say anything or aware that Emily was trying to sort through her feelings. Although Emily had always inwardly questioned how Scott had crashed the car in the first place, dying had not been Scott's choice. She knew that. On the other hand, it had been Dillan's choice to flee Oak Hill, not even letting his brother know he was alive until nearly two decades later.

Without thinking about it, Emily stopped walking again so she could put her arms around Trevor in a tight hug. He seemed surprised, at first, but then he squeezed Emily reassuringly. Awkwardly, he said, "It gets better. I'm sure a ton of people have told you that, but most of them probably don't have quite the firsthand experience that I do."

Emily released Trevor and looked at him earnestly. "It does get better. Sometimes, it's two steps forward and one step back, but I've come a long way from where I was two years ago. Come on; it's almost one."

Soon, Emily found herself stationed at the entrance to the festival, handing out programs and welcoming the arriving attendees. It was the busiest Friday she could ever remember in her years of volunteering at the festival.

Tonight, I'm trying those Tarot cards again. I'm going to keep trying, too, because it's the least I can do for Scott.

Trevor had gotten his brother back, even if he was living several states away. Emily couldn't get Scott back, but she could help find out what was preventing his spirit from moving on, at least.

As the afternoon wore on, Emily found herself thinking less and less about Scott or Robert, and simply enjoying the pleasure of exchanging smiles and greetings with complete strangers. There was something calming in the ritual, a sort of reassurance that she was surrounded by goodness.

By four o'clock, the stream of people coming into the festival was just a trickle, and some dark clouds were steadily marching closer to Oak Hill. The breeze began to pick up, and Emily felt a slight chill. She was pleased when Trish appeared at her side, holding out an umbrella. "Here," Trish said at her usual brisk pace, "just in case."

"Thanks, Trish! I know the forecast wasn't calling for rain today, but it sure feels like it's going to storm."

"Remember, if there's lightning, don't stand out here like an idiot."

Emily laughed. "I promise."

"Hey, by the way, have you seen that photo floating around? That ghost picture?" Trish leaned toward Emily, excited.

"You mean Trevor's cell phone picture? Yeah, he showed me and Sage earlier today."

"Trevor? Williams? No, this was some lady attending the festival. She took a photo of the memorial at Robert Gaines's booth, and there's supposedly a ghost in it!"

Emily had been handing a festival program to a young couple, and now her head whipped toward Trish. "What? Did you see it? What did the ghost look like?"

"I just heard about it. Supposedly, there's a man standing next to the memorial, but you can see right through him! Some people think it's just a glitch, like the lady's camera didn't work right, but of course a lot of people think it's the artist's ghost."

Emily was staring at Trish now. "Trevor got a photo almost exactly like that!"

"Well," Trish continued matter-of-factly, "there's also a rumor that Robert was killed. If that's true, maybe his ghost is trying to tell us who killed him."

Emily had to chuckle. Trish and Jay seemed to be the reigning Gossip Queen and King of Oak Hill, so of course they had both already heard that Robert's death was no accident. Quickly, Emily confirmed the rumor for Trish, but she didn't divulge the things Detective Hernandez had said about the burn marks on Robert's throat. She would let the police announce that when they were ready.

Trish's eyebrows rose to a height Emily hadn't known was possible. "Interesting! Quite a scandal for our humble little hometown arts festival. I've got to get back to the bakery—lots of folks will come in around the time the festival closes—but thanks for filling me in."

Emily waved the umbrella. "And thanks for this! Let's hope we all stay dry!"

Trish bustled off, and Emily was left wondering about this latest photo of Robert's ghost. Why was he showing up in photos? Emily did find some strange amusement in the fact that Robert's art had been altered photographs, and here his ghost was, showing up in photographs. Apparently, even in the afterlife, Robert didn't want to be separated from his preferred medium. But what he was trying to communicate, if anything, was beyond Emily's guess. She would have to take a closer look at Trevor's photo once she was at home in front of her laptop.

When the festival closed at five o'clock, Emily dropped off the few remaining programs at the volunteer tent and made a beeline for Sage's booth. Along the way, she spotted Marianne, who was still hard at work trying to sell some art to an interested-looking woman. The piece looked like a stylized fairy, its hands reaching up in celebration and its wings spread wide. To Emily, the fairy had a slightly bloated, almost clumsy look, and there were no details: it was more the suggestion of a body, and the face was nonexistent. It wasn't the graceful, ethereal type of fairy Emily usually saw depicted in art, that was for sure. It was also a mottled green color, and Emily guessed it was supposed to look earthy. Even as Emily decided that she didn't care for Marianne's style of sculpture, she saw the woman at the booth open her purse and pull out her wallet.

Maybe it's just too avant-garde for me to appreciate it.

Emily arrived at Sage's booth to find the curtain dividing the space closed. She could barely hear Sage's low, nearly monotone voice, which she used when communicating with spirits, and knew her best friend was working with someone. Sage had set up a couple of folding chairs in the front half of the tent as a sort of makeshift waiting area, so Emily sat down, happy to give her feet a break.

Sage emerged about ten minutes later, smiling at a woman who looked like she was in her sixties. "Book an appointment the next time you're in town antique shopping," Sage said, handing over a business card. "I'm sure your sister would love to communicate with you again."

The woman beamed at Sage, thanked her profusely, and walked away. Emily glanced up at the sky and hoped the woman made it to her car before the rain started. The wind was picking up, and a few loose tent flaps shuddered under its force.

"Did you hear about the other photo?" Sage asked.

"The one some woman took? Trish told me."

Sage's eyebrows drew together. "Some woman? No, I mean the one Arnie from the mayor's office took. He wanted to take a photo of the memorial that's sprung up in front of Robert's booth, I guess so he could brag on social media about what a nice town we are or something, but there was a transparent figure of a man in the picture. Just like Trevor's photo!"

"Whoa. Then that's three photos Robert has shown up in today! He must want to communicate."

Sage jerked her shoulders in frustration. "Then he's doing a terrible job of it. I tried to sense him so many times today, but I got nothing. And yet, he's obviously here."

"Weird. Also, a memorial? Really? Trish mentioned it, but I didn't want to believe it. The guy makes Oak Hill look terrible with his art, but now we're supposed to leave flowers at his booth?"

Sage sat down in the empty chair next to Emily. "Between you and me, I think that guy who's been running the booth since Robert died started it, and then people felt obligated to participate and started adding to the pile. Robert's death is the best thing that ever happened to his art career, and the memorial keeps the buzz going."

Emily shook her head disapprovingly. "Not a classy move."

"No, but it's smart from a business perspective."

Smiling mischievously, Emily said, "If you die, can I capitalize on it by hosting séances in your name, promising guests that they'll get to speak to you from beyond the grave?"

"You have my full permission!"

Sage and Emily were still laughing when Trevor walked up. Behind him, a flash of lightning cut through the sky. He held out his phone excitedly. "Have you seen the other photo?"

Trevor's face was flushed, and Emily knew he must have rushed to Sage's booth as soon as he got the photo he was showing them now. She and Sage bent over the phone, peering at the screen. Just like in Trevor's first photo, there seemed to be a man standing in the background that was only half visible. His features were muted, and his clothing simply looked like varied shades of gray. In the foreground, a woman was smiling proudly while holding up what Emily recognized as Selena's little bird feeder.

"Did you take this?" Emily asked.

"No. I overheard the woman and her husband discussing it. They had noticed the ghost, and they were trying to decide if it was paranormal or simply a trick of the light. I showed them my photo, then convinced them to send me a copy of theirs. I told them I'd pass it along to the psychic medium who was working with the police." Trevor gave Sage a wide smile.

"Good work, junior detective!" Sage straightened up and gave Trevor a mock salute. "So that's three other photos we know about. I wonder how many more Robert has appeared in without anyone realizing he was even there?"

Emily took the phone from Trevor's hand and retreated into the back half of the tent, where the shade made the photo easier to see. She held the phone just inches from her eyes and squinted at the image. "It looks like he's doing something with his arms," she said.

Soon, Trevor and Sage were flanking Emily, all three staring at the photo. "You're right," Trevor said, "but like my photo, I think this one needs to be seen on a bigger screen." He promised to email it to Emily as she handed his phone back to him.

A loud crack of thunder rolled across the square, and Emily saw a few of the day's last shoppers running for cover as fat raindrops began pelting them. Over the sound of the rain and the echoes of the thunder, Emily heard a resigned sigh from Sage. "I wanted to go home and take a shower, but it looks like we're going to get a shower here, instead."

"We could make a run for it," Trevor said, but Emily could tell by the tone of his voice that he didn't really mean it. Already, more lightning was forking through the sky, and it was too dangerous to risk dashing to the high school parking lot so they could drive home. The umbrella Trish had loaned Emily would keep her safe from the rain, but not from the lightning.

Sage grabbed one of the chairs from the front of the booth so that all three of them could sit around the table in the back of the tent. She closed the curtain with a flourish, and the confined space was suddenly so dark that for a brief moment, Emily could only see the outlines of her friends. Once her eyes adjusted, she could see Sage reaching into the cooler. As she triumphantly pulled out three cans of soda, Sage said, "We may as well make the best use of this storm."

Emily leaned back and stretched her tired legs out in front of her. "If you had a bottle of wine, I wouldn't say no."

"We're not going to mix business and pleasure." Sage

set the cans on the table, then turned her back to them again to reach into a bag sitting next to the cooler. Soon, she had placed a purple seven-day candle in the center of the table, along with a few sheets of paper, a pencil, a bell, and a silver dollar. As she sat down, she said, "Spirits are a form of energy, and the more energy we can provide them, the stronger they can become. It's why ghosts sometimes drain the batteries in a ghost hunter's camera or cause interference with electrical equipment. Lightning is energy, too."

"You think the storm can help give Robert Gaines a boost?" Emily guessed.

"Exactly. I want to try to contact him again, and maybe the extra energy is what he needs to finally make his presence known."

Emily glanced at Trevor, since he wasn't used to impromptu séances like Emily was. He actually looked excited as he nodded his approval. Sage glanced at Emily, who just tilted her head in a little *why not?* gesture.

Sage lit the candle, then fixed her gaze on a spot somewhere behind Emily. Her eyelids drooped, and her lips began to move with words meant not for Emily and Trevor, but for Robert. Gradually, Sage began to whisper, but it was still too quiet for Emily to make out the words over the sound of the storm. Sage exhaled loudly, then drew in another lungful of air as she closed her eyes. When she spoke again, her voice was louder. "Robert Gaines, we've seen you in photos. We know that you are still here with us. Clearly, there is something you want to communicate. Will you please come speak with us? Come tell us how we can help you."

Sage repeated the invitation three more times, her voice growing louder with each one. Finally, with a frustrated grunt, Sage opened her eyes and threw up her hands. "Nothing! There's just complete radio silence. If his ghost is here, why can't I at least sense it? And if his ghost isn't here, then where did it go? Did he get stuck inside someone's camera?"

Sage had posed the question sarcastically, but she tilted her head thoughtfully. "Is that possible? Can you capture a ghost inside a device like a camera?"

"The Victorians believed you had to cover up photos and mirrors after someone died in the house, or else their spirit might go into one of them and get stuck," Emily offered.

Trevor threw Emily a surprised look. "That's a weird fact to know."

Emily shrugged dismissively. "Not really. I live in a haunted Victorian house. Scott and I once talked about doing a themed weekend where we would recreate a house in mourning, like they used to do in the era the house was built. I did a ton of research, then we never did the event."

"You should," Trevor and Sage said at the same time.

"Maybe someday," Emily said noncommittally.

Thunder sounded again, and it was clearly coming from a different direction now. The storm had very nearly passed over them, and weak sunlight was sneaking through a gap between the curtain and the wall of the tent.

"Let's all go home before we get stuck in another storm! Seriously, I need a shower!" Sage made swatting motions at Emily and Trevor as she shooed them out of her tent. Emily didn't argue; she was eager to go home and look at the two photos Trevor had emailed her. She hoped that seeing them on the larger screen of her laptop might show the ghostly image more clearly.

Sage headed to the registration tent to meet Jen, so Emily and Trevor walked to the high school parking lot together. The air was thick with moisture, and Emily could feel the loose hairs that had slipped out of her ponytail sticking stubbornly to her neck. Suddenly, a shower and fresh clothes sounded like the best thing in the world, and she hoped her guests would linger over their dinners so she could have a little quiet time before they all returned.

Emily said goodbye to Trevor, promising to let him know if she gleaned any new information from the photos as she climbed into her car. She was quickly home since most festival visitors had long since left and the roads were clear of traffic.

Gretchen greeted Emily warmly when she walked in the front door, reporting that it had been a good day with plenty of calls from people interested in making reservations. Emily remarked on the paper bag she spotted sitting on her desk with the Grainy Day Bakery logo on it, and Gretchen explained happily that Trish had just dropped off the baked goods for Saturday morning's breakfast, and she had given Gretchen some leftover biscuits. "People in this town are just so nice!" Gretchen enthused.

Except for the murderers. "They are. It's one of the reasons I love calling Oak Hill home."

Soon, Emily had the house to herself, and she wasted no time in jumping into the shower. Once she had washed off the accumulated dust and sweat from the festival, she pulled on her normal uniform of black jeans and a button-down blue blouse with *Eternal Rest Bed and Breakfast* embroidered in silver on it.

Emily's next order of business was looking at the photos Trevor had sent, but she was disappointed that seeing them in a larger format didn't explain why Robert Gaines was even showing up in them in the first place. In the photo Trevor had taken, Emily could see how closely the blurred face matched that of her former guest. Robert was simply standing in front of his booth, his arms at his sides. He appeared to be staring right at the camera.

In the photo of the woman holding up Selena's painted pottery, Robert's body was turned slightly, and he held his left arm out to his side, almost as if he were pointing at something. If that was indeed what he was doing, then Emily didn't know what he was pointing at, and she speculated that it must be something outside the frame of the picture. She texted both Sage and Trevor to tell them she hadn't had any luck, then turned her attention to catching up on email.

The evening was a nice, relaxing break after the day's excitement. Emily's guests trickled in, all seeming pleased with their sales for the day and ready for a good night's sleep. By ten o'clock, everyone was back, and Emily took it as her cue to retreat into her bedroom. She remembered her earlier promise to herself to break out the Tarot cards again, but her eyelids were fighting to close, and she reluctantly gave in and went to bed. *Tomorrow. I promise.*

The next morning, Emily's guests were out of the house by eight o'clock. They had all breakfasted quickly, saying that Saturdays were usually the best sales days, and they wanted to do any tidying up that might be necessary after the storm of the day before and make sure their best pieces of art were on display.

That left Emily with a full hour before Gretchen was due to arrive for work, so she sat down at the kitchen table with a cup of coffee and the silk-wrapped Tarot cards. She was carefully shuffling them and focusing on her desire to communicate with the ghosts of Eternal Rest when her cell phone rang. She was surprised when she looked at the screen and saw it was Sage calling. Sage was a night owl, and Emily knew that even though Sage had a booth to open at the festival, she would sleep as late as possible before making the short trip from her house to the square.

"What's wrong?" Emily asked in greeting. The same feeling of urgency that she had felt when she had tried practicing with the Tarot cards before was washing over her again.

"Come to my booth as soon as you can," Sage said. "We have work to do this morning."

"What do you mean? What's going on?" Emily realized she was half standing, as if she were subconsciously preparing to dash out the front door.

"My phone has been ringing since last night. As it turns out, Robert Gaines has been hanging out in a lot of photos. Everyone is calling me because I'm the town medium, and they don't know who else to turn to. People are spooked, Em. We need to figure out what Robert is trying to tell us."

"My new assistant will be here at nine, and I'll be walking out the door as soon as she walks in it."

After Emily hung up, she gazed down at the Tarot cards in front of her. Holding her breath, she turned over the top card. It was the Seven of Swords. Emily ran her finger along the guide to the cards' meanings until she found that one. Sage's neat but small handwriting told her the card meant deception.

By the time she greeted Gretchen quickly and gave a hurried explanation about needing to go help a friend with her booth, Emily was still mulling over the meaning of the card. Did it have to do with one of the ghosts at Eternal Rest, Scott, or Robert? She was still thinking about it after she had parked in the high school parking lot and walked to the square.

Emily completely forgot about the Tarot card as soon as she turned down the row where Sage's booth was located and saw the crowd of people standing in an anxious knot.

15

As Emily got closer to Sage's booth, she could see that many of the people gathered there were holding photographs in their hands. Some people were waving theirs excitedly while others were holding their photos with an expression of uncertainty. Emily worked her way slowly through the tight knot of people, and she could hear some of them commenting on her presence as she moved. She caught the words "Eternal Rest" and "haunted" several times.

Sage was standing at the front of her booth, the flap of the tent already open and two elderly ladies seated on the chairs. They, too, held photographs in their hands.

"So many?" Emily asked as soon as she caught Sage's eye.

"Every one of them has a photo of Robert. I just can't figure out what he's trying to tell us."

Sage waved Emily into the back of the tent, announcing over her shoulder that she would be with everyone shortly. As soon as she had closed the curtain to have some privacy, Sage said with a note of worry, "This isn't good, Em. Some people are excited, but most are scared. You know word about this is going to spread like wildfire through the festival today. Jen's eyeballs got bigger every time my phone rang last night. It's great publicity for my business but not for the festival."

Emily gazed at the curtain as she pictured the people on the other side. "Have everyone write their name and contact information on the back of their photo. Oh, and when they took the photo. Maybe, if we look at them in chronological order, we'll find some kind of pattern. Have everyone leave their photos with you, and promise them that you'll keep them posted on anything you find. That way, they aren't waving those things in front of everyone's faces at the festival today."

"Good idea. Okay, I'll do that while you call Detective Hernandez. He needs to know what's going on."

Emily agreed, and soon she was on the phone with Danny, who sounded surprised when Emily told him just how many people had shown up with photographic evidence of a ghost.

"You get ghost hunters at Eternal Rest often, correct?" he asked.

"Lots. And if you're thinking that it's extremely rare for a ghost to show up in one photo, let alone twenty or so, then you're absolutely right. This is—"

"It's extraordinary," Danny broke in. "I'll come by and take a look at the photos later."

Emily wrapped up her call with Danny and was just emerging from behind the curtain when she noticed the young man who was now handing Sage a photo. He looked familiar, and Emily gazed at him as she tried to remember where she had seen his brown eyes and shoulder-length brown hair before. He mumbled something to Sage, and Emily was only able to hear the word "evidence."

Did this man know she and Sage were working with the police? As he turned away, Emily realized he had been the one comforting Jess at Tuesday's volunteer meeting. Emily glanced at the photo that Sage had now put on top of her growing pile, and she saw it showed the altered photo of Jess. The man had taken a picture of it hanging in Robert's booth, and she wondered if he had been documenting the piece of art to present the argument that it should be removed because it shed Jess—his girlfriend, Emily surmised—in a bad light. He was collecting evidence, not for a murder investigation but to build a defamation suit or something similar.

Emily helped Sage collect the final photos, and soon it was just the two of them standing there. Sage looked at the few photos sitting on the top of the pile and said, "I'm going to figure out a way to hang these up so we can look at them all at once. I don't know if we'll find a pattern, or some kind of secret message, or what, but I want to look at the big picture, so to speak."

"Good plan."

"In the meantime, I'd like a breakfast burrito with sausage and extra salsa. And a coffee with extra sugar, of course."

Emily blinked at Sage. "Am I cooking you breakfast?"

"No, silly. You're getting it to-go from The Depot. I've been so swamped with calls about these photos that I haven't had breakfast yet, and I'm starving. You can grab some cash out of my wallet."

Emily smirked at her friend. "I'll go, but I'm only doing it because you're hard at work on a police case!"

"You're hard at work on a police case, too," Sage said, looking at Emily seriously. "Staying well-fed is important when you're on the hunt for a killer!"

By the time Emily returned from The Depot with a bag full of food, Sage had strung several rows of rope along the back wall of the tent, and she had clipped the photographs to them with clothespins. The open flap of the tent wasn't allowing in much light, and as Emily was unpacking the food, Jen came by with a portable spotlight. "Sage, here's the—ooh, hey, Em, you got breakfast?" Jen set the light down and began to reach into the bag.

"Wait for your turn!" Emily said playfully. "Sage asked for a breakfast burrito, but I added to the order. There's a spinach and cheese omelet in here for you, and a Southwestern scramble for me." Emily pulled the final Styrofoam container out of the bag and presented it to Jen like a gift.

"You're a lifesaver. Thanks!" Jen's expression turned grim. "How bad is it? This ghost situation, I mean."

Emily shrugged. "I've never seen anything like this. Maybe two or three ghost hunters have taken photos at Eternal Rest that seem to show something paranormal, and even then, I couldn't say with absolute certainty that they caught one of my ghosts on film. Robert Gaines definitely wants us to know something. The good news is that he's just showing up in photos. No one is in danger, of course."

"Of course." There was a hint of doubt in Jen's tone.

As Jen hustled back to the registration booth with her food, shouting another thanks over her shoulder, Sage plugged the light into an extension cord and set it on the table so that it was aiming right at the back wall of the tent. Emily and Sage both sat down with their food, facing the wall and eating in silence as they gazed at the photos, hoping to find some message in them.

Emily couldn't find any sort of meaning.

After taking the last bite of breakfast, Emily stood and started to examine each photo closely, one at a time. Robert's ghost was easy to spot in each one. In some, he was simply looking at the camera. In others, he seemed to be pointing at something. The direction he was pointing varied depending on the angle from which the photo was taken. As she studied the photos, Emily could hear Sage behind her, murmuring quietly as she sought to feel Robert's presence.

In the photo that showed the altered image of Jess, the ghost was pointing toward something outside the frame. Emily unclipped the photo and looked at the contact information on the back. The young man's name was Caleb Watson, and Emily surmised he was part of the expansive Watson family that lived on the east side of Oak Hill. The Watsons had several farmhouses along one road, and locals jokingly referred to it as the Watson Compound.

Finally, after staring at the photos for nearly half an hour, Emily realized there was, in fact, a pattern. In each photo that showed Robert pointing or turned away from the camera, his arm or his body was always directed toward the front right corner of the tent, where a large wire display rack held a collection of his altered photographs. In some of the photos Emily was looking at, the rack wasn't even in the picture, but the ghost was still pointing in that direction.

As Emily became more convinced that her conclusion was correct, she began to flip each photo up to see when it had been taken. The earliest ones, from the hours after Robert's death, showed a display rack that had a blank spot directly in the center. Later photos showed that different pieces of art had been hung there, presumably being replaced as each one sold. The other pieces of art hanging on the rack changed, as well, and Emily knew the man running the booth in the wake of Robert's death must be digging out every single available piece to keep up with the rapid pace of sales.

That blank spot, though, the one that had been so

prominent in the earliest photos, was exactly where the altered photo of Eternal Rest had been hanging prior to Robert's death. For some reason, the ghost of Robert Gaines was trying to draw attention to his artwork of Emily's home.

"But why?" Sage had asked the question three times, after Emily had anxiously interrupted her to explain her suspicion that Robert Gaines was appearing in photos so he could call attention to his artwork of Eternal Rest.

"I don't know," Emily said, also for the third time. "But don't you agree that of all the pieces hanging on that display rack, that's the most likely piece he would be pointing at?"

"Not necessarily," Sage answered. "The piece isn't even there in the photos, so it would make more sense that he's pointing at one of the pieces that's still hanging up." Sage looked closely at one of the photos. "Look, there's the fire department. He must have had several of his Oak Hill pieces grouped together here. Maybe he's trying to tell us that someone killed him because of one of these."

Emily gave a short, self-conscious laugh. "You're right. I'm jumping to the conclusion that any murder must involve my home, but of course that's ridiculous. So, let's say you're correct: Robert's ghost is pointing at a photo of Oak Hill that he altered, one that offended someone so much that they killed him over it. Where do we even begin to find a suspect?"

"I guess we figure out which Oak Hill landmarks are represented in those pieces, then go from there. Hopefully

Detective Hernandez has a magnifying glass and a good eye, because I'm passing this job on to him. I know he was going to stop by, but the lighting at the police station will be a lot better for looking at these photos. Why don't you take them to him? The festival is already open, so I need to get to work to make up for the time I lost yesterday."

Emily agreed to walk the photos to the police station. As she emerged from the sea of tents, she saw a line of people snaking along the sidewalk, slowly moving through the festival entrance. Emily walked without really paying attention to where she was going, lost in thought about the meaning of the photos. Even though Sage was probably right, she couldn't shake the feeling that Eternal Rest did have something to do with this. Emily couldn't even pinpoint why that would be the case, and yet her instincts were telling her that, somehow, her home was directly involved.

Maybe not my home but my guests.

As expected, Danny was interested in the information Emily had gleaned from the photos, and he promised to let her and Sage know anything they might learn from the artwork on the display rack. By the time Emily returned to the festival, though, her mind was made up: she was going to act on her hunch.

Sage was already hidden behind her curtain with a customer when Emily returned to her booth and took a seat in the front section of the tent. She bounced one leg nervously as she developed a plan in her mind. When Sage emerged from her makeshift consultation room and sent her customer off with a few words of encouragement about how loved ones enjoy checking in on the living, Emily stood abruptly, anxious to get the idea out before she second-guessed herself. "Sage, I know it will sound nuts, but please listen. My gut is telling me that Robert was pointing at the spot where the photo of Eternal Rest had been hanging. I don't know why he wants to draw attention to my house, but he does. Maybe one of my guests killed him. Maybe he just wants to hang out with my ghosts so he can get some advice on the afterlife. Who knows? Either way, since we haven't been able to speak to him here at the festival, let's try speaking to the ghosts at Eternal Rest. Maybe they know something or can help us figure out a way to communicate with Robert."

Emily stopped, out of breath, and looked at Sage with trepidation. Instead of being shot down, like she expected, Sage simply said, "Okay."

It took Emily a moment to realize Sage was agreeing to her plan. "But... Oh. You're okay with that?"

"Yes, of course. Why wouldn't I be? I'm the one telling you that you need to develop your skills, and listening to your gut is a big part of that. If you feel a séance at Eternal Rest is the right thing to do, then let's do it!"

Emily hadn't realized how tight her shoulders were until she felt them relax. "Thanks, Sage. Even if the ghosts don't know anything, it will make me feel better to have at least tried that path."

Sage smiled. "I'm going to keep sending messages out to him, even though I have yet to sense his presence again. I'll invite him over to your place."

"I'll check in with you later," Emily said quietly, noticing two very interested-looking young women walking up to them. "Have fun with your customers!"

With a couple of free hours before her shift, Emily decided to wander down each row. She said good morning to Jake and Selena, then stayed for a while to admire the oil painting Jake was working on. She knew he must pull in a lot of interested shoppers by showing off his skills with a live painting session. The painting showed a crumbling log cabin that was slowly being covered by long tendrils of kudzu. The painting was both beautiful and a little sad at the same time, at least to Emily. There was a certain poignance about someone's home being reclaimed by nature.

Emily's feelings were much different when she stopped by Marianne's booth. She idly picked up a small blue sculpture of a bird—at least, that's what Emily thought it was supposed to be. She held it close to her face, trying to feel some connection to Marianne's artistic style, but there was nothing. Still, when Marianne shouted a hello in her direction, Emily politely smiled and complimented the artist on the number of people browsing her work.

Greg was located one row over from Marianne, and his booth was every bit as crowded. He looked uncomfortably large inside the white tent, his head bent as if he were afraid of hitting one of the metal beams supporting it. He nodded at Emily and continued speaking in quiet tones to someone who was gesturing at a bust that looked like it had come from the Ancient Greece exhibit at a museum.

Emily's day at the festival sped past, thanks in large part to how busy she was giving directions and local dining recommendations to out-of-town visitors. She couldn't remember ever seeing the Oak Hill Arts Festival so busy. Saturdays were always crowded, but this beat anything in her memory. Several people asked her about the murder, but no one mentioned the ghost. Emily wondered if Robert was done posing for photos or if the festival was so crowded that no one noticed the translucent figure lurking in the background.

In what felt like a short while, Emily found herself back at Eternal Rest. Gretchen had heard the gossip about the ghost, and she jumped up from the desk chair as soon as Emily walked into the parlor. "Have you seen a photo of the ghost? Does it mean that artist was murdered? I wonder who it could be!" Gretchen's hands were clasped together in front of her chest, and she looked at Emily eagerly.

Emily put her purse down and stretched her arms over her head. "As a matter of fact, I've seen about twenty photos of the ghost. We don't know what it means, but the police are working on it."

The front door closed with a bang, and soon Marianne's voice boomed from the parlor doorway. "Oh, you're home already. I've got to change because I managed to rip my skirt earlier. It goes all the way up, so I've been keeping my backside hidden as well as possible all day. I'm going to change before heading back into town."

Emily could see the startled expression on Gretchen's face and resisted the urge to laugh. "Okay," Emily said to Marianne, deciding to ignore the subject of her clothing altogether. "Just so you know, I have a friend coming over tonight. She's a psychic medium, and we'll be doing a séance in the dining room."

"Oh! Do you normally have those?"

"Usually, it's just a special event one night a month, but we think the ghosts here might have some insight for us."

Marianne reached up and scratched her head thoughtfully. "Insight about what?"

Emily opened her mouth to explain the ghostly photographs and her hunch that, somehow, Eternal Rest was involved, but she caught herself, remembering that she needed to regard everyone under her roof as a suspect. Thinking quickly, Emily said, "We have reason to believe the spirit of my late husband needs my help, but for some reason, he's unable to communicate. We've been trying to get the ghosts here to share anything they might know."

Marianne looked at Emily uncertainly, her expression cycling through sympathy, confusion, and something that looked like disapproval. "Oh," she finally said. "Good luck, then." With that, Marianne turned and headed upstairs.

Gretchen was bouncing in her excitement as Emily turned to her again. "A séance! Wow! So, there's a ghost at the festival, but you're going to talk to the ghosts here instead? Why not try to talk to the artist?"

"My friend Sage has been trying, but apparently, he'd rather be seen and not heard."

"Oh, of course! Because he's an artist! I bet you could sell those photos for tons of money!"

Emily mumbled something about the photographers owning the images, not her, and ushered Gretchen out the front door as quickly yet politely as she could. Gretchen was doing well so far, and she seemed to be a nice young woman, but until it was time for the séance, Emily needed a break from talk of ghosts.

Now, there was only one other person in the house. Just as Emily was wondering how long it would be until she would have a little time alone, Marianne came thumping down the stairs. "And there she goes," Emily said quietly to herself.

Emily called goodbye to Marianne, who shouted, "I'll see you later!" The firm clang of the front door closing told Emily that now she did have Eternal Rest to herself.

She also had work to do before her guests showed up, like unloading the dishwasher and wiping down the dining room table. Reluctantly, Emily got up and headed for the kitchen. As she moved down the hall, she could see something on the floor, just outside her bedroom door.

It was a Tarot card.

Emily felt her hand shake slightly as she bent down to retrieve the card, wondering how it had escaped both the silk wrapping and her nightstand drawer. The card was the Five of Wands, and Emily stared at it as she went into her room and fished Sage's guide out of her nightstand. *Conflict, rivalry*, Sage had written.

Emily had no idea what that could mean.

Sage arrived at seven o'clock, the bag full of her séance tools in one hand. Emily was pleased to see Reed standing right behind her. He was dressed surprisingly well for a casual Saturday night at Eternal Rest, wearing a pair of black trousers with a midnight-blue Oxford shirt. Emily noted his silver cufflinks and wondered if Reed had a date after the séance.

"Yes, I know," Reed said pointedly to Emily as he walked in the front door. "I look very handsome. And yes, I do have dinner plans after this."

Emily pointed a finger at Reed. "You claim it's your cousin who has the well-developed sixth sense, but I think it runs in the family."

"I saw you eyeing my cufflinks, that's all." Reed gave Emily a teasing smile.

"Sure."

Sage had already emptied the contents of her bag

onto the dining room table by the time Emily went in and shut the door behind her. She wanted to ask Sage about the appearance of the Tarot card and how it might have happened, but she wanted to wait until the two of them were alone. At the moment, though, Reed was already sitting down opposite Sage, and Emily flicked off the lights before settling into a chair next to her best friend. The purple candle gave everyone's faces a soft glow.

Since it was just Emily and Reed, who were familiar with Sage's way of conducting a séance, Sage didn't bother to explain what she was doing. She immediately addressed herself to the empty space in the middle of the table, calling Robert's name. When that availed nothing, as expected, Sage called on Mrs. Thompson. The elderly lady quickly made her presence known, knocking on the wall behind Sage and Emily.

"Mrs. Thompson, is there a new ghost here?" Sage asked.

Emily's former assistant knocked twice on the wall, which was Mrs. Thompson's way of saying *no*.

"Have you heard about a new ghost here in Oak Hill?"

No.

Now, Emily spoke up, saying, "Mrs. Thompson, I know you like to keep an eye on our guests to make sure they're happy. Have you overheard any of them saying anything suspicious?"

No.

"Have you seen any of them acting strangely?"

No.

Emily fell silent, not sure what else to ask. If Robert Gaines was trying to draw attention to any of her guests, then Mrs. Thompson, at least, hadn't noticed anything out of the ordinary in their behavior. Next, Sage called on Kelly Stern. Kelly typically preferred to use automatic writing to communicate, guiding Sage's hand as she held a pencil poised over a blank sheet of paper.

Kelly was quick to respond to Sage, writing her greeting in large letters. As soon as she knew Kelly was present and eager to communicate, Sage said, "Kelly, have you seen a new ghost here at Eternal Rest?"

Sage went through the same questions she had with Mrs. Thompson, and she continued getting the same negative responses. Then, Sage surprised Emily by asking, "Kelly, the last time I asked you about Scott, you wouldn't tell me much. Are you willing to share more now?"

At first, Emily thought Kelly would refuse to answer the question. Sage's hand was perfectly still for a full minute, and Emily felt a wave of anxiousness wash over her. Why was Kelly always so hesitant when it came to telling them what was going on with Scott? Kelly was the one who had first alerted Emily to the presence of Scott's ghost, but since then, whenever Sage or Emily tried to get more details, Kelly would remain stubbornly silent.

Finally, though, Sage's hand did begin to move. Instead of Kelly's usual large, bold letters, the writing was small, almost timid. *He's so close. Can't get through. Too weak.*

Sage's eyes stayed fixed on the paper as she read the words out loud. "Kelly, what can't he get through?"

Don't know.

"Is there some sort of barrier around Oak Hill? Like a psychic wall?"

Maybe.

"But you've seen him?"

Yes. Close, but not clear.

"Do you know why he's weak?"

No.

During this entire exchange, Emily had felt her shoulders and chest tightening. The same feeling she had gotten while looking at the Tarot cards before was closing around her, a sense of urgency that she felt almost like a physical force.

So when the front doorbell rang, Emily was so tense and ready for something to happen at any moment that she jumped, trying to stand while pushing her chair back from the table at the same time. Instead, she lost her balance and fell sideways, landing hard on her knees.

Reed leapt out of his chair and ran to Emily, taking her hands to help her up. "Are you okay?" Reed gripped her fingers tightly and looked intently into her eyes. She knew he wasn't just inquiring about her physical well-being.

"I'm not sure," Emily said honestly. "Let me get the door, though."

Emily dashed to the door and flung it open. She was surprised to see her mother standing there, a worried look on her thin face. "Mom? What's wrong?"

Even as she spoke, Emily looked down and saw that Rayna Ward was holding a black frame. Slowly, Rayna turned the frame around, and Emily found herself staring at Robert Gaines's altered photo of Eternal Rest.

Rayna's voice was shaking. "I think this photo I bought is haunted."

Emily looked at her mother, down at the photo, then back up at her mother. "Mom," Emily said slowly, fighting to keep her voice even. Her brain was racing with thoughts about murder and Scott's spirit and how much her knees were beginning to sting, and she fought to find a sense of calm. She wasn't entirely successful. "Why the hell do you have that awful photo?"

Rayna jerked backward as if Emily had struck her. "Awful? It's your own house! Your bed and breakfast, that your grandparents worked so hard on! I bought it as a present for you."

Emily bit her lip, realizing her error. "I'm sorry, Mom. I didn't mean to snap at you. It's just... I got really upset when I saw that photo at the festival, because it makes our ghosts look so evil and tortured. Robert Gaines just made me mad when I commented on it, and then he wound up dead, and we don't know who could have possibly murdered him in the middle of the festival, and—"

Rayna shook her head, her gray bob swinging. "No, he couldn't have been murdered! I heard the rumor, too, but it seems terribly unlikely."

Emily realized her mother was still standing on the front porch, the photo clutched in her hands. She stepped back and waved Rayna inside. "Come on into the dining room. Sage and Reed are here, too."

Rayna complied, carefully placing the framed photo in the middle of the dining room table as she greeted Emily's friends. Her voice was shaking again. This time, though, it wasn't from fear but from hurt. "I thought Emily would like it," she told Sage and Reed sadly.

Sage got up and rubbed Rayna's back sympathetically. "It's okay. You caught us at a weird time, and I'm sure Emily will change her mind about it once she sees it hanging up in a spot with a lot of natural light."

Emily threw Sage a grateful glance. She would never like the photo, and she would eventually have to find a gentle way to tell her mother that she would never, ever hang it up in her house, but she appreciated Sage trying to soften the blow of Emily's reaction. Clearly, her exchange with her mother had carried into the dining room.

"Mom, you said you think the photo is haunted," Emily prompted, pulling a chair out for Rayna. "Let me guess: you see a gray figure that looks like a person, but you can see right through it, and the features are muted, like they're not all there."

"I see a figure, yes, but he's all there. Look." Rayna leaned forward and put her finger on the glass covering the photo. She was pointing at one of the floor-to-ceiling parlor windows, and Emily could clearly see the man who was standing in it. He wasn't transparent at all, and she could see every detail, right down to the horrified expression on his face.

It was definitely Robert Gaines.

18

"It looks like he's part of the photograph," Sage said. "All of the other ghosts are clearly painted in or pieces of paper that have been pasted in place, but it looks like he was standing right there in the parlor when this photo was taken."

"Why is Robert's ghost haunting the photo of my house?" Emily frowned at the image.

"Because your hunch was right," Sage said, sounding like a teacher praising her student. "Robert Gaines was showing up in all of those other photos in an effort to draw our attention to this piece of art. The question, of course, is why?"

Emily's eyes flicked to Reed's. "I have to wonder if one of my guests has something to do with Robert's murder."

Reed laughed softly as he shook his head in disbelief. "Are you accusing my dinner date of murder?"

"I'm not checking anyone off the suspect list unless they have a rock-solid alibi," Emily said, a note of apology in her tone. "Remember, I thought Mr. Williams was a nice man, and then he nearly killed me and Sage."

"After killing Kelly Stern and then trying to murder his own sons," Sage interjected.

"Exactly. And then I thought David Neal was an okay guy, even if he did work with that jerk Jaxon, and he turned out to have killed three people." Emily laughed self-consciously. "I'm not a great judge of character, so no matter how nice someone seems, they're staying on my list of potential killers."

Now Reed's expression was serious, no trace of a smile remaining. "Be careful, Emily. You're talking about people's lives and reputations here. You could do a lot of damage if you falsely accused someone."

"I'm not accusing anyone," Emily said, holding up her hands defensively. "I'm just saying that I'm not giving anyone a free pass simply because they have a sunny disposition."

Emily's mother had remained silent during this exchange, her head swiveling from one speaker to the next as her mouth slowly opened wider and wider. Finally, she stood up, her hands on her hips. "Emily."

Suddenly, Emily felt like a teenager again, coming in half an hour after curfew. Only her mother could utter her name in a way that conveyed disappointment, anger, and even fear. Emily's eyes dropped to the surface of the table, which only made her look directly at the pained visage of Robert Gaines, or whatever piece of him was now occupying the photo of Eternal Rest.

"Emily," Rayna said again, but this time her tone was almost pleading. "Why are you even involving yourself in this? It has nothing to do with you. Even if, somehow, one of your guests had something to do with this artist's death, that doesn't mean you have to go around trying to figure out which one of them it was. It's dangerous." Rayna's voice broke on that last word, and Emily felt her heart lurch. She hadn't stopped to consider how scary her recent connections to death might be for her family.

But, Emily had to admit to herself, her mother was making some good points. *Why do I feel like I have to get involved in this? Because Robert was once a guest here? Because he created that awful altered photo of my house? Because Detective Hernandez asked me and Sage to help out?*

No. None of that. Even as Emily ran through those possible explanations in her mind, she knew the real answer to her mother's question.

"Because, Mom," Emily said softly. "I don't know how to help Scott's ghost. I couldn't help him after he died, and I still can't. But if I can help another ghost, even if it's someone I didn't really like, then I'm going to do it."

Rayna sat back in her chair, a shocked expression on her face. "Scott's ghost?"

Emily bit her lip as she felt tears spring to her eyes. Rayna still believed Scott had simply died in a car accident, and she didn't know that Reed's cousin had been visited by Scott's ghost in a dream where he asked her to tell Emily he needed help. Emily knew her mother had loved Scott like her own son, and she hadn't meant to tell her about her fears for Scott's spirit. At least, not like this. Emily turned to Sage, afraid that if she spoke, she might start crying.

Sage gently, quietly filled Rayna in on the signs they had gotten that Scott hadn't crossed over yet and that he needed their help to find peace. She also relayed the final conversation Emily and Scott had shared before his car accident, in which he told Emily they needed to explore ways to protect Eternal Rest spiritually. As Sage wrapped up by sharing Emily's belief that Scott's car crash hadn't been a simple accident but had somehow been directly related to what he had told her in that last phone call, Rayna began crying softly.

Emily was by her mother's side in a heartbeat, her arms around her as she felt her own tears begin. "I'm so sorry, Mom," she whispered. "I didn't want to tell you. I didn't want you to worry about me or about Scott."

Rayna reached up and squeezed Emily's hand. "I

worry about you every day, dear, and I've been worrying about you even more since all of this business with Benjamin Williams." Sitting up straighter, Rayna wiped at her cheeks with her free hand. She squared her shoulders and nodded her head decisively. "You have a big heart, Emily, and if that extends to helping ghosts, then I'm not going to tell you to stop. And if there's anything I can do to help you help Scott, then count me in."

Emily just squeezed Rayna's shoulders tighter and mumbled, "Thanks, Mom. I love you."

"I love you, too, dear."

Sage clapped her hands together. "Great!" she said brightly. "That means we'll have another person who can join us for séances!"

Rayna's expression changed to surprise. "Oh, I don't know about that. Emily's dad would think I'd lost my mind."

Emily chuckled as she released Rayna and straightened up. "He doesn't mind that I do it."

Now Rayna chuckled, too, as she replied self-consciously, "I guess it's a night for sharing secrets, then. He's always been a little, well, uncomfortable with you so actively trying to talk to the ghosts here. He says he knows it's harmless, but it goes against all the fire and brimstone preaching he grew up hearing."

"Oh, he must love it when I come to visit him!" Sage didn't sound embarrassed at all. Rather, she sounded delighted at the idea of shocking Emily's dad.

Reed had been silent during all of this, but now his voice cut through the room. "Look at the photo."

Emily glanced down, expecting to see it moving on its own or something similarly dramatic. She saw nothing out of the ordinary. "What are we looking at?"

Then she saw it. Or, rather, she didn't see the figure of

Robert Gaines standing in the parlor window. He had disappeared.

Everyone in the room gasped in unison. Emily reached out and touched the now empty spot. The glass felt oddly cold against her fingers. "He just left the photo? But where could he have gone?"

"Maybe…" Sage was looking all around, as if Robert might pop up in a corner of the dining room and say hello. All heads turned toward her.

"Maybe, what?" Reed prompted.

"He's been showing up in photos, trying to indicate this very piece of art," Sage said. By her slow, thoughtful tone, Emily knew Sage was still trying to work out the details. "I felt Robert's presence right after he died, but since then I haven't felt a thing. Some part of him is showing up in photos at the festival, but maybe the bulk of his presence went into this picture. Why, I don't know. It could have been an accident, or maybe he did it because he remembered that Eternal Rest is haunted, and he thought he could talk to the ghosts here. By putting himself in the photo of Eternal Rest, all we had to do was transport the photo here. You did that part for us, Rayna."

"And now Robert is loose in my house," Emily said.

"I don't know if I would phrase it that way," Sage said. "Rather, Robert is now free to communicate with the ghosts here at Eternal Rest. By that logic, your idea that Robert was trying to accuse one of your guests of killing him might not be correct. He simply wants help from your ghosts."

Emily had to admit she liked that idea a lot better.

Now, Sage was all efficiency. "Em, get the lights. Rayna, just sit there, and remember not to whisper, so we don't all think we're hearing ghostly voices. Reed, you know the drill."

In seconds, everyone was seated around the dining

room table again, the purple candle shining eerily onto the photo of Eternal Rest. Sage repeated her pleas for Robert's ghost to come communicate with them, and Emily's body tensed in anticipation.

Nothing happened. Just as before, Sage's continued invitations went unanswered. Finally, she swore. "I don't even sense his presence. He has to be here, though! If he left the photo, then where else could he have gone?"

Reed was looking at his watch. "And where could Kat have gone? Our original plan was to leave for dinner five minutes ago, but if any of the artists have come back, then they must have come in the door really quietly."

As Reed walked into the parlor to call Kat, Sage blew out the candle and began to pack away her séance tools. She was still grumbling about Robert not showing up to talk. Emily turned on the lights and picked up the Eternal Rest photo, wondering where she could put it that it would stay safe—in case Robert's ghost decided to haunt it again—but out of sight. She looked apologetically at Rayna. "Mom, it's going in the hall closet for the time being. I hope you understand that with everything going on involving Robert Gaines, I'm not big on staring at this every day."

"Honestly, you won't hurt my feelings by hiding it away. I thought I was giving you a neat gift, but now it's looking like I gave you a clue to help you solve a murder. Seeing that man pop up in the parlor window gave me the creeps, and I'd rather not see anything like that again."

Emily gave her mom a grateful look. "Thanks for understanding. While you're here, would you like to stay for dinner? I'm not going to make anything fancy, but I'll even send you home with leftovers for Dad."

Rayna and Emily were walking down the hallway when the front door opened. Emily turned and saw Kat, Marianne, Jake, and Selena all crowd through the door.

Jake had a brown paper shopping bag gripped tightly in one arm, and he gave a triumphant shout when he spotted Emily. "We're celebrating! Join us!"

Emily couldn't help but smile back. "What are we celebrating?"

"All four of us had phenomenal sales today," Selena said. "We got champagne to celebrate."

"Honestly, we started celebrating about an hour ago," Kat clarified, throwing Reed an apologetic look. "Sorry. I lost track of the time. Can we have a quick toast before dinner?"

Marianne plucked the bag out of Jake's arm. "I'll handle this while you all fill Emily and her company in on our day."

Emily gave Marianne some quick directions to the champagne glasses, then followed everyone into the parlor. Kat was already telling the group, though she was looking only at Reed, about the regional magazine that had done a photo shoot of her art installation at Hilltop Cemetery that morning. "And then, this afternoon," she continued, "my booth was constantly full of people. I've never had such a great day at a festival. Not just this festival, mind you, but any festival, ever."

By the time Marianne came into the parlor with a tray of champagne-filled glasses, Selena was recounting how popular her pottery had been. She expected to be completely sold out of it by Sunday afternoon.

As Marianne plucked a glass off the tray and handed it to Emily, she said loudly, "Not only did I have big sales, but I sold big things! My largest sculptures sold today, and of course they have the highest prices, so I really made out."

Emily noticed how much Rayna was enjoying this unexpected celebration, and she knew that her mom would be telling all of her friends in Oak Hill about her evening hanging out with some of the artists.

Jake raised his glass, and the others followed suit. "To an absolutely fantastic day at the Oak Hill Arts Festival!"

Everyone leaned in and clinked their glasses together. Just as Emily raised her glass to her lips, though, she heard a loud thud from somewhere else in the house, like something had been thrown hard to the floor.

"Excuse me," Emily said, slipping away from the group. The others were all happily chatting, though, and if they had heard the noise, they seemed unconcerned about it. Emily doubted anyone but Sage and Rayna noticed her departure. She put her champagne glass down on a side table and stepped into the hallway.

Emily stopped and listened, wondering if she would hear the sound again. She hadn't been able to tell where it came from. When she didn't hear anything, she poked her head into the dining room, but everything looked fine there. Nothing had fallen over in the kitchen, either.

As soon as Emily walked into her bedroom, she knew the sound had come from there. The wedding photo of her and Scott, which normally hung above the bed, was lying on the floor near the bathroom door, about twelve feet away from its usual spot.

Something had thrown the photo across the room.

Emily rushed over to the photo, not at all concerned that a ghost had probably done this, but worried that her wedding photo had been damaged. Surprisingly, for as loud as the noise had been, the glass was still in one piece. Emily sighed in relief and sat down next to the photo, wondering if this paranormal activity had to do with Robert or with Scott.

Leaning over the photo, Emily inspected every inch as she looked for a sign of Robert's form in it. When she determined it was empty of any unexpected visitors, she relaxed and took a moment to appreciate Scott's bright smile and the excitement in his green eyes. Emily was laughing in the photo because she had just tossed her bouquet, and it had flown right to her widowed great-aunt, who had sworn for years that she was better off alone. Emily and Scott had posed for picture after picture that day, both before and after the wedding ceremony, but it was this candid photo that they had loved the most. It showed them, the real them, enjoying life and sharing a special moment with their loved ones.

A little knock made Emily look up. Sage was standing there, her champagne glass in her hand. "Is that what made the noise?"

"Yeah. Not a scratch or a crack on it, but it somehow traveled all the way over here from above the bed."

"Huh."

"That's about as far as I've gotten in my assessment, as well. Is this about Scott or Robert? Or is Kelly throwing a fit because she's too young to drink champagne with the rest of us?"

Sage laughed. "I'm going to guess Robert, since we know Scott is still stuck out there, beyond the mysterious barrier that's keeping him from visiting you. But I'm glad you mentioned Kelly. Before I leave tonight, I'm going to ask your ghosts to be on the lookout for Robert. I want to know anything they might see or experience that's out of the norm."

"I'm making dinner, if you want to join us."

"No, I'm heading home. Jen got takeout for us. Reed and Kat just left, and I think the rest of the artists are actually going out to dinner."

Emily made a surprised expression. "I figured they would just 'celebrate' all night."

"Jake only bought two bottles of champagne. He might be a great artist, but he's a terrible party planner. You want help hanging that back up?"

"It's a one-person job, but thanks. And thanks for coming over, even though we only wound up with more questions. Have a good night, and I'll see you tomorrow."

"Cheers!" Sage said, raising her glass toward Emily before draining it.

Eventually, Emily got up and rehung the photo, taking extra care to ensure it was straight. She felt reluctant to rejoin her jubilant guests. She was happy for their success, of course, and pleased they were so quick to include her in the celebration, but she felt too weighed down by what Trevor would call "ghost stuff" to really enjoy the moment. By the time she quietly returned to the parlor, Selena had picked up the tray and was collecting empty glasses.

"Care to join us for dinner?" Selena asked.

"No, thanks. Mom and I are going to have a quick bite here. You three have a good time."

"Oh, we will!" Marianne said loudly.

"Here, I'll take the tray back to the kitchen." Emily reached out and deftly lifted the tray from Selena's hand. She waved at the three guests as they walked out the front door, already discussing whether they would have time to stop by Sutter's for a drink after they ate dinner. With her free hand, Emily plucked her glass off the side table, sniffed it, and wrinkled her nose. She had never been a big fan of champagne, and the smell of this stuff only served to prove Sage's pronouncement that Jake had the right idea but poor execution. She poured her glass down the drain as soon as she got to the kitchen.

Emily made turkey burgers while Rayna sat at the table in the corner, sipping slowly at the last of her champagne.

They avoided talking about ghosts while they ate, and Emily's mind was feeling more settled as she sent her mom out the door with a container of food for Emily's dad.

As Emily fell asleep, she found herself unexpectedly wondering about Greg Van Breda and whether he had also enjoyed a successful day. It was a shame he was the one guest who wasn't part of the celebration, but then, Emily realized, maybe he wouldn't have been comfortable in the middle of such a happy, energetic crowd. He didn't seem like the type to enjoy a party, even if it was just a little impromptu one in the parlor of Eternal Rest.

The alarm clock on Emily's nightstand showed that it was a few minutes after midnight when her celebratory guests returned. Greg and Kat had both come back quite late, too, and Emily could tell by each artist's tread on the wooden floors that Greg had beat Kat back to Eternal Rest by only thirty minutes. Emily tried to picture Greg out on a date with a local resident, but she just couldn't form the image in her mind. She would inevitably wind up picturing a pretty woman sitting at a table with Lurch from *The Addams Family*.

Since she was such a light sleeper, Emily had woken up every time her front door had opened. Even with her curiosity about the haunted Eternal Rest photo and Robert's sudden appearance and disappearance from it, she still fell easily back to sleep every time, too tired out by the events of the past few days to stay awake, even if her brain was begging to review every little detail again and again.

Emily actually woke up feeling refreshed on Sunday morning, and she had put the breakfast trays and carafe of coffee on the sideboard in the dining room long before anyone else had come downstairs.

At five minutes before nine, Emily was still the only person downstairs. Gretchen arrived a few minutes early for her shift, and as Emily waved her in the front door, she pointed over her head. "I can hear them moving up there, but no one has shown up yet. I expect we have at least a few hungover guests this morning."

"Did they spend their evening toasting to that artist who was killed?" Gretchen asked.

"Actually, they were celebrating because they all had killer sales yesterday." When Gretchen giggled, Emily realized her unintended pun. Embarrassed, she said, "*Great* sales, I meant."

Gretchen was nodding. "My husband heard the same thing from a couple of artists who came into the store where he works. They said they sold tons of art, even though no one could stop gossiping about that dead man. Apparently, his death has been really great for business."

As she spoke, Gretchen's face was as expressive as her tone. Emily wondered if she was mentally practicing for an interview on some true crime documentary about Robert Gaines. Emily could just picture it: "I didn't know the man, but his ghost came to visit my workplace…"

"Oh, that reminds me!" Emily said, knowing Gretchen would readily agree to what she was about to request. "It's possible the ghost of that artist is here at Eternal Rest, and I need your help looking for any signs of his presence." Quickly, Emily told Gretchen about the photo and how her best guess was that Robert's ghost had jumped from the photo of Eternal Rest to the real thing.

Gretchen enthusiastically promised to be vigilant all day. She actually jerked backward at the sound of footsteps on the stairs, but she quickly blushed and relaxed when Selena and Jake appeared.

"Morning," Selena said, yawning. "We're running late. Any chance we can get some coffee to go?"

"Of course. Let me guess: after dinner, you headed to Sutter's?"

Jake just groaned in response.

Emily dug through some things in the sideboard before pulling out a stack of Styrofoam coffee cups, flourishing them with a triumphant, "A-ha!"

Selena winced at the sound.

Emily let them pour their own coffee while she retrieved some brown paper bags from the kitchen so they could pack up a few baked goods.

Kat was in the dining room when Emily returned, and she was already filling a Styrofoam cup. "Did you have a nice time last night?" Emily asked, trying to keep her tone neutral.

"Oh, yeah," Kat said, right before taking a big bite of a bagel, presumably so she couldn't answer any more of Emily's questions.

Marianne bustled into the room, a little subdued compared to her normal state, but still loud. "Oh, I'm paying for it today," she announced as she began to fill a bag with croissants. "What a good time last night."

As soon as those four guests were out the door, Emily heard Greg's heavy step in the hallway. She turned to find him staring at her. "Good morning," Emily said brightly, forcing herself to meet Greg's eyes instead of avoiding his intense gaze.

Greg just nodded. "They came back late last night."

"Yes. They were out celebrating a good day of sales."

"That's not respectful to you."

Emily shrugged. "They weren't that late. I don't mind."

Greg set his lips in a tight line and drew his eyebrows down, as if he were scrutinizing Emily. "I was out a little late, too, but I tried to be quiet."

"And I appreciate that, Greg. Thank you. I hope you had a nice time out in Oak Hill last night."

"I had a pleasant evening."

Greg poured himself a cup of coffee, not into a Styrofoam cup but a porcelain one. He sat down at the table and directed his gaze out the front window, clearly done with the conversation.

By Emily's calculations, Greg finally left with just enough time to drive to Oak Hill, park, walk to his booth, and maybe even pull aside the front flap of his tent before the festival opened.

Gretchen was settled into the desk chair, so Emily got her cleaning bucket and headed upstairs to neaten the guest rooms. As she cleaned, she spoke out loud to her spectral residents. She especially addressed Kelly, asking her to write down anything unusual that might indicate the presence of another ghost. "We're trying to help this guy out, Kelly. And if you've already met him, you probably know he's a little arrogant, but you've met worse. And the sooner we help him, the sooner he'll be out of our house!"

Gretchen was busy answering the phone all morning, but Emily had a few moments to relax after she got done with the guest rooms. Soon, though, it was time to head downtown for her afternoon volunteer shift.

Sunday was always a busy day at the arts festival, even if it wasn't quite as crowded as Saturday. Emily had planned to pop into Grainy Day Bakery to see how Trish was doing, but the line snaking out the door told her everything she needed to know. Trish would be exhausted but happy by the time she dropped off Emily's order for Monday morning's breakfast. Emily could have easily picked up the baked goods after the festival each day, but she suspected Trish preferred delivering the order to Eternal Rest on her way home, as usual, so she could catch up on gossip without worrying that customers might overhear.

From the bakery, the easiest way to get into the festival was through a side entrance. The route to the volunteer booth took Emily right past Robert Gaines's booth. She walked up to the front of the tent, peering in to see if any other Oak Hill photos were still for sale. A tall, gangly woman stepped in front of Emily, her diamond earrings sparkling. She spoke in a clipped, businesslike tone. "Hi, there. What piece are you interested in?"

Emily blinked at the woman. She had expected to see the man who looked like a lawyer again, and before she could think, she blurted out, "Oh, you're new here."

"I just arrived last night. Brian said he needed extra help today."

"Brian?"

The woman jerked her head toward a man at the back of the tent, and Emily realized it was the same man who had been selling Robert's art since the murder. "My lawyer. My husband is dead, but his art is thriving. Now, which piece are you interested in buying?"

Emily stared at the woman, stunned. She thought her mouth might be making some kind of noise, but she knew it wasn't actual words, because she had no idea how to respond to an announcement like that. Finally, after several attempts, Emily managed, "I'm sorry for your loss."

The woman sniffed as she shrugged her shoulders dismissively. "We were about to get divorced. That sneak has been stashing away cash and artwork, hoping it would go unnoticed so I wouldn't get my fair share. Now that he's dead, I can sell his art and get what I deserve. So, in the end, I'd say I won."

Surely she didn't kill her husband. If she had, she wouldn't be bragging about getting her due right now.

That thought was quickly followed by another one: *Don't trust anyone.*

If she shouldn't cross people off the list of suspects just because they seemed to be nice, Emily reasoned, then she couldn't discount people who seemed to have such an obvious motive.

Just as she was thinking that, Emily felt someone shoving their way past her. A man pushed her out of the way with his shoulder, not violently but still firmly enough that she had to move her feet quickly to refrain from stumbling.

Once Emily was certain she wasn't going to topple over, she glanced up to see who was being so rude. It was the young man who had helped Jess at the square, the same one who had taken a haunted photo of the art featuring Jess. Caleb Watson, Emily remembered.

Now, he was glaring at Robert's widow. "Why do you people insist on keeping this booth open?" he said through gritted teeth. "His art isn't welcome in this town."

Undaunted, the widow crossed her arms over her chest and returned the man's stare. "Really? Because the number of pieces we've sold and the prices people are happy to pay tell a different story. Are you going to buy something?"

Caleb sneered at her. "Of course not."

"Then get out of my face and out of my booth."

Caleb's arms twitched as he leaned forward. "This is not over." He spun on his heel and stalked away, pushing past several people and causing every head in the immediate area to turn and stare after him.

The widow watched him until he was out of sight, then she rolled her eyes and made a disgusted noise. Her head swiveled toward Emily. "Well? Which piece do you want to buy?"

"No, thanks," Emily mumbled as she turned away. Her feet were already moving before she realized she was following Caleb. She caught up with him at the edge of the festival, where Jess was leaning against the trunk of an oak tree. He stalked over to her, and although Emily couldn't hear him or see his face, she knew from his wild gesturing that he was recounting his experience. Jess's body seemed to shrink as she hunched her shoulders and wrapped her arms around herself. Her head drooped, and she kept her eyes fixed on the ground below. While Caleb was clearly angry, Jess herself seemed embarrassed and maybe even a little sad.

Emily stopped and watched them for a moment. Her first thought was that she would say something to Caleb, though whether it would be commiseration or an accusation of murder, Emily wasn't sure. She could perfectly understand both his and Jess's feelings over Robert's art, but clearly, they were taking it even harder than she had.

With a little shake of her head, Emily turned and made her way to the volunteer booth. She was grateful she had arrived at the square early, or she would have been late checking in for her shift.

Before long, Emily was stationed at the assistance tent. She had just reluctantly told a curious couple which artist had died and where his booth was when she saw a flash of bright pink out of the corner of her eye. Knowing it was Sage, Emily said, "How goes it with the ghosts today?" as she neatened a stack of festival maps on the table in front of her.

It wasn't Sage's voice that answered, "I think the question is, 'How goes it with the dead today?'"

Emily looked up and was surprised to see Danny Hernandez next to Sage, a grim expression on his face. For a split second, Emily thought someone else had died, but Hernandez clarified, "We got the full report back from the lab. If you have a few minutes, I'd like to discuss it with you two."

It was easy to be excused from volunteer duty since it was at the request of a detective with the Oak Hill Police Department. Plus, Emily figured, the volunteer supervisor was probably hoping that whatever Danny had to disclose, Emily would bring back details about it.

Danny led Sage and Emily to a booth on the far side of the festival, which was being used as a central point for the various police officers and security people working the event. Roger Newton was there, and he chuckled as Emily walked up. "Miss Emily, are you still involved in this murder case? Surely the ghosts at your B and B don't have anything to say about an artist who died here in the square."

"You're right, they don't," Emily agreed. "I'm hoping the ghost of Robert Gaines will have something to say, though."

Roger harrumphed grumpily, but Emily caught the faintest gleam of amusement in his eyes.

A few metal folding chairs were already sitting in a loose circle in a back corner of the tent, and Danny motioned for them to sit. He teetered on the edge of his chair, leaning in and keeping his voice so low that Sage and Emily had to lean in just as much.

"Up until now," Danny began, "there was a chance Robert Gaines died by accident. A slim chance, but it was possible that he ingested the toxic substance that killed him by mistake. He could have also ingested it intentionally."

Danny paused, and Emily impatiently prompted him. "But now…"

"The lab report has identified the substance as something called polyester resin. It left burn marks from his mouth all the way down to his stomach. It must have felt awful, but he didn't ingest a lot of it. It was probably in something he ate or drank for lunch that day: he was found around lunchtime, and his stomach contents back up that idea."

Emily and Sage both shut their eyes and made sounds of disgust.

"The amount was enough to be lethal," Danny continued, "but it appears the killer wanted to make sure the job was successful. Our coroner here had already identified injection marks on the victim's body, and the lab found more of the polyester resin at those sites. Injecting the substance into the bloodstream was even deadlier than ingestion."

Sage raised a hand, as if she were in a class. "Then why bother to put it in his lunch?"

Danny frowned. "This is where it gets weird. It's possible the killer wanted him to suffer, or maybe they simply weren't sure the ingested substance would do the job. It appears the injections were made after the victim had died, or when he was very close to death. The substance didn't travel all that far from the injection site, indicating his circulation was extremely slow or nonexistent."

"Does that mean the person who did it sat there and watched him die, just so they could do it a second time for good measure?" Emily spoke around the fingers she had pressed against her mouth.

Danny looked at Emily sympathetically. "Probably. I know, it's not a pleasant mental image."

"Wouldn't Robert have tasted the stuff in his lunch?" Emily asked.

"Honestly, I don't know." Danny sat back finally and crossed his legs. "I have no idea what polyester resin tastes like. I doubt many people do. It's used for a lot of things—it's basically a plastic that starts out flexible, then hardens as it cures—but there are strict guidelines about working with it since it's deadly. Because it's a common substance, figuring out where it came from is going to be tough."

Sage had an expectant little smile on her face. "The real question, Detective Hernandez, is why are you telling me and Emily this information?"

"Because I want you to ask Robert's ghost about it. With specifics like this, it might help you communicate with him."

Emily and Sage exchanged a quick glance. "I still can't make contact with him," Sage began.

"But we do think we know where he is," Emily broke in. She and Sage told Danny about the mysterious figure in the photo of Eternal Rest, and how it had disappeared after the photo was brought to Emily. "I've asked my ghosts to keep an eye out for him," she concluded, "but so far, we haven't had any signs of a new haunting."

Emily was surprised when Danny gave her a wide smile. "Say that last part again," he prompted.

"We haven't had any signs of a new haunting."

"No, before that. You've asked your ghosts to keep an eye out for him, but have *you*?"

Emily gasped as Hernandez's words sank in. "We're going about it the wrong way! Robert isn't going to knock on walls or do automatic writing. We have to look for him in pictures."

That means the wedding photo was thrown across the room by Robert, not by Scott or one of my ghosts.

"I can't believe we didn't think of that." Sage rested her head in her hands. "I've been trying so hard to contact him with my usual methods that I never stopped to use his methods. He was an artist who altered photos, so of course he's still expressing himself through photos in the afterlife."

"Let's try asking him questions while we take pictures around the house," Emily suggested. "Maybe we can display the alphabet somehow so he can point at the letters in photos and spell out messages."

"Or we put a map of Oak Hill on the table, and ask him to point out where his killer is now." Sage had her ankh pendant clutched in one hand, her fingers turning it over and over as she thought. "It's been a long time since I tried a new way of spirit communication. This is exciting!"

"Do we want to do this tonight?" Emily asked.

Sage dropped her necklace and spread her hands. "Why not right now?"

21

Even though Sage was so excited, she immediately expressed doubt about heading to Eternal Rest right that moment. "This festival doesn't have a friends and family discount for booths, so I need to keep mine open to make some money," she explained.

Emily was nodding. "And I have my shift until the festival closes for the day."

"There are plenty of volunteers here," Sage said firmly. "They can spare you."

"What's the point in me going if you won't be there to conduct this?"

Sage reached over and squeezed Emily's arm. "You're going to do it, of course. Robert already showed up in a photo of your house, and he used to be a guest. You've got more of a connection with him than I do—I never even met him. This will be great practice for you!"

Emily blew out a loud breath. She looked at Sage, then at Danny, who didn't seem at all adverse to the idea. "But what if I fail?"

"So what if you do?" Sage pointed to herself. "Do you think I'm successful every time? No, of course not. If you don't have any luck getting Robert's ghost to show up in some photos, then we'll try again."

I can do this. The more practice I get, the better chance I'll have of finding a way to help Scott.

"Detective, are you coming, too?" Emily asked.

Danny smiled apologetically. "Unfortunately, no. Remember, working with ghosts is well outside the scope of normal investigating. I can't participate in a professional capacity. But I do think the sooner you attempt to communicate with the victim, the better. Today is the last day of the festival, and artists will begin leaving town tonight. If one of them is the guilty party, I'd like to know before they take off."

Emily was absolutely certain this was something she didn't want to do alone. She thought about asking Gretchen, but she was hesitant to try contacting a spirit with someone she barely knew. She also didn't want to let any calls about reservations go to voicemail. Her mind made up, Emily stood and put her hands on her hips. "Fine, I'll go, but you're going to have to get another festival volunteer out of their obligations for the afternoon."

Danny gave Emily a little wink. "You'll have to use your own powers of persuasion for that. Like I said, I'm not acting in an official capacity. I never even said a word to the volunteer coordinator who let you leave your post. Luckily, she made her own inferences about my presence."

"All right. Wish me luck." Emily looked at both Sage and Danny seriously. "I'll do my best, but I can't make any promises."

Sage stood and put a supportive arm around Emily's shoulders. "You'll be fine. Trevor will be there to help you, and you know he's faced worse than a ghost who pops up in photos."

"How did you…?"

Sage struck a dramatic pose and tried to give Emily a mysterious look, but she couldn't suppress her laughter.

"Of course Trevor is the volunteer you're going to take with you. Who else would it be?"

"Oh, right."

"Also, being psychic gives me some insight into what you're thinking, and you're absolutely right: you should also call Reed and ask him to join the two of you. I don't think you'll need spiritual protection for dealing with Robert's ghost, but it doesn't hurt to have someone who knows about the subject at your side, just in case."

Danny looked at Emily curiously. "Were you really thinking that?"

Emily nodded. "I really was. Welcome to being friends with Sage. Don't think about your deep, dark secrets when you're in her company!"

"You've got this," Sage said firmly.

"And thank you," Danny added.

Emily felt like she was in a daze as she walked to the volunteer booth. She couldn't believe Sage and Danny trusted her to do something that could be so integral to finding Robert's murderer. At the same time, she felt an unexpected thrill.

Over those feelings, though, another one was fighting for dominance inside Emily's mind: urgency. That same feeling she kept getting when she used the Tarot cards was coming over her now, and she didn't know if it was because of what Danny had said about the need to solve this murder investigation before the artists left town, or if it was something else making her feel like she was running out of time.

Lost in her thoughts, Emily was inside the volunteer booth before she even realized she had arrived. She blinked a few times and looked around, but Trevor wasn't among the people there. She found a volunteer coordinator and inquired about his location; she was told he was now taking a turn handing out programs at the entrance.

Emily hastily sought an explanation for why she wanted to take him away from his volunteer work, and after several awkward moments, she said she had a problem at Eternal Rest, and she needed help with it. She mentioned Trevor had once been her assistant, implying he had firsthand knowledge that made him the only person who could possibly help her.

As Emily wrapped up, she realized everything she had just said was absolutely true. Trevor's experiences during his short time at Eternal Rest really had given him an understanding of what she was about to undertake, and if she couldn't have Sage by her side for this, then having Trevor and Reed there with her was the next best thing.

Trevor was chatting with several people Emily vaguely recognized from her high school days as she approached him at the entrance to the festival. The determined look on her face must have been a signal to Trevor that something serious was going on, and he quickly wrapped up his conversation and turned his full attention to Emily.

"Your volunteer shift is done for the day because I've been given permission to borrow you." Emily paused a moment, then added, "If you're willing, of course."

"Are we looking for ghosts?" Trevor raised his eyebrows.

"Just one ghost. Specifically, the ghost of Robert Gaines. I'll fill you and Reed in on everything, if you're in. I'm heading back to the house right now for a little experimental spirit communication."

Trevor made a scoffing sound. "Of course I'm in. Let's go!" He instantly turned to another volunteer, handed over the stack of programs he had been giving to arriving visitors, and made a quick excuse for his departure.

As Emily and Trevor walked to the volunteer parking lot, Emily pulled out her cell phone and called Reed. By the background noise she heard when Reed answered, she guessed he was at the festival, too. "Where are you?" she asked.

"I'm helping Kat at her booth."

Emily knew Reed couldn't see her surprised expression, and she kept her tone even as she said, "That's sweet of you. If you're able to get away, I could use some help at the house. Detective Hernandez would like us to look for the ghost of Robert Gaines. Unofficially, of course."

Reed sounded confused as he responded, "You're going to Eternal Rest to look for the ghost right now?"

"Yes. I'll explain when we're all there."

"Hang on." Emily heard some muffled talking before Reed said, "Okay, I'm on my way."

As she hung up her phone, Emily realized how relieved she felt to have both Trevor and Reed undertaking this effort with her. She knew the two of them would support her and give her a boost of confidence.

Trevor drove right behind Emily to Eternal Rest, and as the two of them walked inside, they saw Gretchen standing in the middle of the parlor, her back to the door. She was shifting her weight anxiously from one foot to the other, and her voice sounded strained as she spoke to someone on the phone. "Sure, I can check on those dates for you," she was saying. "Give me just a minute to get into the reservation system. It's been glitchy today."

Gretchen lowered the phone, took a deep breath, and did a funny little hop-run across the parlor to the desk. There, she nestled the phone between her shoulder and her ear, then began tapping away at the laptop's keys, not even bothering to sit down. In fact, she seemed to be standing as far away from the desk as possible, bending over at the waist and stretching her arms out to reach the laptop. "Yes, ma'am, we do have those dates open. Would you like to go ahead and reserve your room?"

Emily and Trevor had moved quietly into the parlor,

watching the unfolding scene and exchanging confused glances. As soon as Gretchen finished taking the reservation and hung up the phone, she straightened up, keeping her back to the room. Her eyes were directed at the wall in front of her as she said, "Emily, is that you?"

"Yes. Gretchen, what's wrong?"

Gretchen finally turned around, and Emily jerked backward at the sight of her ashen face. "It's been a really weird day, Emily. This house is haunted."

Emily's forehead furrowed. "Yes, I know. We discussed that when you started working here, and you didn't seem too concerned about it."

"Because you said I might hear footsteps or some knocking noises."

"What's been happening instead?" Emily moved slowly toward Gretchen, afraid of startling her, and pulled out the desk chair. "Please, sit. You look like you might faint."

Gretchen looked at the chair with distaste. "I'm not going to sit anywhere near that laptop."

What's wrong with my laptop? "Okay, then come over here and sit on the sofa. Do you want some water?"

Gretchen moved cautiously to the sofa and sat down heavily. She declined Emily's offer, instead leaning her head back, her eyes closed. She sighed, then suddenly opened her eyes and looked at Trevor. "Hi, I don't know you. I'm Gretchen."

"Trevor. Hi. You're Emily's assistant, right? I used to have your job." Trevor gave Gretchen a smile that looked both friendly and sympathetic, but it only seemed to upset her more.

"What? Emily told me about Mrs. Thompson, and of course everyone knows about Trip Ellis. She didn't mention you." Gretchen was looking at Trevor suspiciously.

Trevor glanced at Emily, one corner of his mouth

turned up. "Gee, didn't my time here mean anything?" His sarcastic tone turned serious as he addressed Gretchen again. "I only worked here for a couple of weeks."

"Why only a couple of weeks?"

"Um, well…"

"Trevor's dad has been going through some stuff, so it didn't work out for him to stay here," Emily supplied.

Suddenly, Gretchen's eyes lit up in recognition. "Trevor Williams, right? Your dad is… Oh, I'm sorry. It's probably not something you like to talk about."

"It's not, but it's okay. I know everyone in town likes to gossip about it." Despite his reassurance, Emily could see the stiff, uncomfortable way Trevor was holding his arms at his sides. She knew talking about it with a friend, like Sage, was one thing, but discussing it with a stranger was another.

"For now, though," Emily said firmly, "let's get back to what you've been experiencing, Gretchen."

Gretchen sat straight up, speaking again in the same clear manner that Emily had heard her use previously. This time, though, her eyes were directed toward Trevor. All signs of her fear disappeared as she took on what Emily was already starting to think of as her true crime documentary persona. "Let's start with the photos. About three hours ago, I heard a really loud bang, like someone had dropped a bowling ball upstairs. I ran up there, and a photo in the hallway was lying on the ground. It wasn't damaged, so I put it back. I figured it had just slipped off the nail somehow. Then, about twenty minutes later, there was another big noise. It came from the dining room, and a photo that I think is supposed to be on the fireplace mantel was on the opposite side of the room."

"Did you see anything strange in these photos?" Emily interrupted.

Gretchen frowned. "No, they looked normal. Like I

said, nothing was damaged. But photo after photo wound up on the floor, all through the house, and every time, it sounded like they had been thrown really hard. I thought that was bad, but then—" Gretchen gave a yelp as the front door opened.

In a moment, Reed strode into the parlor. "I got here as fast as I could," he said, looking around as if he might see something amiss. Emily noticed he was clutching something tightly in one hand.

"Gretchen was just telling us that something keeps throwing the photos hanging on the walls onto the floor."

"That's odd."

"Actually, it's not, but we'll get to that in a moment. Gretchen, you were saying?"

Gretchen flashed a smile at Reed, and she seemed to enjoy being the center of attention. She drew herself up, jutted out her chin proudly, and said, "Your laptop is haunted."

22

Emily narrowed her eyes and glanced over Gretchen's shoulder, toward the rolltop desk. "What makes you say that?" she asked.

"I was reading an article online in between phone calls, and suddenly the screen started to"—Gretchen splayed her fingers and wiggled them—"sort of fizzle. It made me think of an old-fashioned TV with static. I thought it was just a bad connection or something, so I didn't worry about it. It happened a few more times, but I wasn't that concerned. Then, it happened again, but this time, there was something *in* the static. Like a shape. It was gone so fast, just a flash, that I barely had time to realize what I had seen. When it happened again, I knew I hadn't been imagining things: there was the image of a man in the static. Just a head and shoulders. He was sort of made of the static, like darker lines that formed the shape, so I couldn't see any distinct facial features."

Emily got up and hurried to the desk. She kept her eyes fixed on the laptop screen as she sat down. "Is he still in there?"

"I don't think so. I saw him a few more times, and then the static stopped."

The tip of Emily's nose was nearly touching the screen. "Where are you?" she whispered.

"Emily, would you like to explain what's going on?" Reed wasn't one to be afraid of ghosts, but his voice had a concerned edge.

"Sit down, and I'll explain everything. You too, Trevor."

Once everyone was sitting, Emily stood in front of them, between the two front windows. She felt like a teacher lecturing her class. "We know that Robert Gaines was murdered with a toxic substance. We think his ghost is trying to communicate with us, hopefully to help us find his killer. Sage has been trying to communicate with him, but she can't sense his presence at all. However, his ghost has been showing up in photos and even in his artwork of Eternal Rest. We think his ghost is here now."

Even though she had heard this before, Gretchen still let out an excited little squeal. Her hands were clasped together. Reed and Trevor simply looked at Emily with curiosity.

"The fact that photos keep falling off the walls confirms our theory: Robert isn't haunting the house, but the photographs in it. What we're going to attempt now is to take our own photos. If we invite him to come appear in them, and ask him some questions, then maybe we'll get some kind of response."

Reed was nodding. "I'm not a fan of Ouija boards, but if you had something like that, he could point at letters and spell out his message in photos."

"We were thinking the same thing. I'll write the alphabet on some sheets of paper, and we can spread them out on the dining room table."

To Emily's surprise, it was Gretchen who spoke up. "You said you believed Robert's ghost came here so he could communicate with the ghosts of Eternal Rest. I think you're wrong, Emily. He wants to communicate with you. Otherwise, he would just talk to the ghosts, right? He wouldn't need to be throwing around your photos."

"But why would he want to communicate with me? He was a guest here once, but we weren't friends. I certainly don't have any insight into who killed him."

"He knows you believe in ghosts, so he trusts you'll look for him and listen to whatever he might have to say," Reed said. "Robert knows you're someone who can connect the living and the dead."

As if to punctuate Reed's statement, a loud crash sounded behind Emily. Instinctively, she hunched her shoulders and threw her arms over her head before realizing the sound had come from the ground. She whirled around and saw the painting of her grandparents lying on the floor. She lifted it and replaced it on its hook, mumbling, "That's not even a photo, but I get it, Robert. We know you're here."

"This is so exciting," Gretchen said, her voice barely above a whisper. Now that she wasn't alone in the house, her fear seemed to have been replaced by enthusiasm.

"Before we try getting Robert to spell anything, let's see if he'll even show up in our photos. Everyone take out your phones and split up. I'll go upstairs. Reed, you take the dining room. Trevor, you go in the kitchen." Emily shook her head. "No, swap that. Trevor, given your previous experience in my kitchen, I don't want you in there looking for a ghost. Gretchen, you take photos in here, but if the phone rings, grab it. I want all of you to invite Robert to come appear in your photos. Snap as many as you can, and let's see if we get anything."

As Reed stood, he extended his hand toward Emily, and she saw he was holding a small glass vial filled with something reddish.

"Is that dirt?" Emily asked.

"Graveyard dirt, to be specific," Reed said. "From my

great-great-grandfather's grave. I dashed up there to collect it before coming here. You know I have faith in the ability of our ancestors to protect us spiritually, and having a little dirt from their burial site can help amplify their efforts. Paul Artemis Marshall is on the case."

Emily smiled gratefully as Reed's fingers closed over the vial again. "Thank you, Reed. I don't think Robert's ghost is dangerous, but when he's throwing photos around, I don't want to take any chances. We'll find a way to honor Mr. Marshall for his help."

Reed was smiling, too. "I think Kat already did that with her portrait of him."

"Then I'll be sure to thank her." Emily returned her attention to the others. "Okay, let's do this!"

Emily went upstairs and stood in the middle of the hallway. She could hear Gretchen's faint voice drifting from the parlor. Lifting her cell phone in front of her, one finger on the camera button, Emily said, "Robert, if you're up here with me, I want to help you. Please appear in my photos. I'm going to start right now."

On that last word, Emily began clicking. She took about twenty photos, continuing to call out to Robert, then stopped to look at what she'd gotten.

There was nothing. All she saw in the photos was her ordinary hallway.

Emily tried a second time, taking another string of photos while imploring Robert to show up in at least one of them. Again, though, she captured nothing paranormal in the images.

Wondering if the others were having better luck, Emily went downstairs and checked in each room. All of them reported the same lack of success.

Frustrated, Emily walked to the hall closet and pulled out Robert's framed photo of Eternal Rest. She peered at it intently, wondering if Robert was in there somewhere.

He definitely wasn't in the parlor window again, and Emily looked everywhere else, even checking the cemetery part of the photo for a sign of his presence. Grumbling, she replaced the photo and shut the closet door harder than intended. The bang echoed down the hallway. "Where are you, Robert?" She nearly shouted the words, tired of playing this strange, ghostly hide-and-seek with him.

Emily realized she was listening hard and had to remind herself that Robert wouldn't be making any noises in answer.

Or maybe he is.

When Gretchen and Reed had both suggested that Robert wanted to come to Eternal Rest not for its ghosts but for Emily herself, the portrait right behind her had been thrown to the floor. And after the failed séance, it was a photo of Emily that had been thrown across her bedroom.

Robert was moving photos in an attempt to communicate. At least, that was Emily's speculation. She took a few steps down the hallway and turned to face a framed photo of the house as it looked when her grandparents had first opened Eternal Rest. "Robert, if you can hear me, please make this photo fall down."

Emily stared hard at the photo. At first, there was nothing, then she detected what seemed to be a slight vibration. She shut her eyes and opened them again, unsure if she was really seeing the frame moving. Yes, it was definitely vibrating, and soon a quiet, rapid *tap-tap* could be heard as the movement increased, and the frame began to bounce against the wall. A few seconds later, the frame didn't just fall; it looked like it was being yanked down by unseen hands. It crashed to the wooden floor with a loud bang, though the glass remained perfectly intact.

"Oh! Thank you, Robert! Now we're getting somewhere!"

"Emily, everything okay?" It was Reed's voice, and Emily turned to see his head poking out of the kitchen doorway.

"Yes! I just asked Robert to make this photo fall if he could hear me, and he did it!"

"That's great. Hang it back up, and let's ask him some more questions."

As Emily complied, the others gathered in a tight knot around her. "Robert," Emily said once the photo was on the wall again, "that was really great. We want to help you find your killer. If that's why you're here, then make this photo fall again."

Just as before, the entire frame began to vibrate, almost imperceptible at first, then growing to a crescendo before the photo was pulled off the wall.

Gretchen and Trevor both gasped. Reed said, "Explain our plan to him, and ask him if he's able to do what we're asking."

Emily checked the photo and was relieved to find it was still undamaged. Once she returned it to its hook, she said, "Robert, we want to use our cameras to communicate with you. You wouldn't show up for any of us earlier, and I'm not sure why. Are you able to appear in our photos?"

The photo remained perfectly still.

"Why not?" This time, Emily wasn't directing the question to the ghost, but to the people gathered around her.

"What's different about the photos we're taking compared to all the photos he appeared in at the festival?" Trevor asked. He sounded as confused as Emily felt.

"He was standing in front of his booth in those," Emily answered, "but we know he's here, so the location shouldn't matter."

"Maybe it's not the location that matters, but the content of the photos," Reed suggested. "His artwork was in all of the festival photos. It seems like Robert is only showing up in his own art, or in a photo that shows his art. Or, for some reason, your laptop."

Gretchen spoke up, her tone embarrassed. "Actually, the article I was reading online was about Robert and his art. There were a lot of pictures of his work."

"Is that it, Robert?" Emily directed her voice to the photo. "Are you only able to appear if your own art is present?"

The photo on the wall began to vibrate again, the frame dancing against the wall.

A low hum began to sound, seeming to come from each end of the hallway, as well as from upstairs. It grew louder as everyone looked around wildly, instinctively drawing closer together.

The photo crashed to the floor as bang after bang sounded through the house. Then, suddenly, everything was silent.

"I'm going to say your guess is correct," Emily told Reed. Her voice was shaking slightly.

"Yeah." Unlike Emily, Reed's voice sounded interested rather than scared.

"At least it's easy to test that theory," Emily continued. "We'll put Robert's photo of Eternal Rest in the dining room, take a bunch of pictures of it, and see what happens."

Emily had tucked her cell phone into the back pocket of her jeans, and when it rang, everyone jumped, then laughed.

It was Sage. She didn't even say hello but instead yelled, "What happened just now? I felt a huge wave of spiritual energy coming from out your way."

When Emily filled her in, ending with Robert bringing down what she assumed was every single photo in Eternal Rest, Sage responded, "See? I knew you could do it!"

"We haven't really done anything, yet."

"You've established contact and gotten a form of yes-no questioning underway."

Emily realized with a start that Sage was right. She had been so skeptical of being able to do what Sage and Danny had suggested, so doubtful of her burgeoning abilities, and yet, she had begun communicating with Robert's ghost without really thinking about it. She had been too busy simply trying to get some answers to even realize what she was doing.

Before Emily could communicate any of that, Sage said, "Now get back to it, but keep me posted about any details that you find!"

Emily promised, though she half expected Sage to know anything they learned without the need to explicitly tell her.

As the group headed for the dining room, Emily got the altered photo of Eternal Rest out of the hall closet and carried it with her. She still found it as distasteful as ever, but she was, at least, grateful it might help them catch Robert's murderer.

Emily grabbed a stack of plates off the sideboard and put them in the middle of the dining room table, then leaned the photo against them so it was upright. Trevor removed the chairs from one side of the table so they could all get unobstructed photos of Robert's art.

"Robert, we're ready. I hope you are, too," Emily began. "If you can understand me, please show yourself in some of our pictures. Ready? Now!"

Everyone began snapping, the room nearly silent as they stared at their phone screens and concentrated on taking photo after photo. After about half a minute, Emily called a halt to the activity.

"Let's see if anyone got anything," she said.

"Oh, oh, look!" Gretchen shouted. She handed her phone to Emily. "He's just on the other side of the table!"

Gretchen was right. The gray form of Robert Gaines's ghost could be seen standing between the dining room table and the front windows. Emily could see right through him to the curtains behind.

"Fantastic, Gretchen! Anyone else?"

There were a few moments of silence as everyone

scrolled through photos and carefully searched each one. It was Reed who finally spoke up. "Here, I got him in one, too. He seems to be pointing straight ahead." Reed looked up at Emily. "I think he's pointing right at you."

Unable to figure out what the proper response was to being singled out by a ghost, Emily just said, "Anyone else?"

Only the two photos showed Robert. All of Emily's had been perfectly normal.

The four of them tried again, and this time, it was Trevor who was rewarded for his efforts. Robert was still there on the other side of the table, but he seemed to be leaning over it.

"If he wants to talk to me, then why isn't he showing up in any of my photos?" Emily mused.

The photo of Eternal Rest tipped forward and fell facedown on the table.

Trevor jumped, then looked at Emily sheepishly. "Sorry. After my previous incidents with your ghosts, I'm a little skittish."

"What kind of incidents?" Gretchen asked.

"One of the ghosts here tried to kill me."

Gretchen's mouth formed a perfect *O*. "Am I in danger here?"

Trevor realized what he had done and hurried to say, "No, not at all. It was the ghost of"—he paused awkwardly—"of the girl my dad killed. She's not a mean ghost, but she had me confused with him. She knows who I am now, and I'm pretty sure we're on good terms with each other." Trevor glanced upward. "Right, Kelly?"

Emily set the Eternal Rest photo upright and spoke loudly to Robert. "You seem to want to talk to me. Why aren't you showing up in my photos, then?"

"Emily, what does Sage like to remind you about when you're communicating with Mrs. Thompson?" Reed was trying to sound stern, but Emily could hear the laughter in his voice.

"That I have to ask yes or no questions," Emily answered sullenly. She directed her attention to the general area she thought Robert's ghost was occupying and tried again. "Robert, are you not showing up in my photos because you don't want other people here with me?"

The photo fell over again.

"I'll take that as a *yes*."

"How did you guess?" Trevor asked.

"I thought maybe having four cameras pointed at him might be distracting, even confusing."

Trevor put his arm on Emily's shoulder. "We will be right outside, in the hallway. Be careful."

Reed didn't say a word. He simply put his container of graveyard dirt down on the dining room table with a decisive *thunk*.

Gretchen was bouncing on the balls of her feet again as she walked into the hallway. Before it had been from nerves, but now it seemed to be from excitement.

Maybe I should offer her the job permanently. She's friendly, she seems reliable, and she's cool with the ghosts when they're not possessing my laptop.

Reed was the last one out the door. As he closed it, he looked at Emily and gave her a reassuring nod. Even though she was doubting herself, she knew Reed had complete confidence in her ability to get some answers from Robert.

Once she put the Eternal Rest photo back into place, Emily held up her phone again. "It's just me now, Robert. Can you pose for my camera this time? On the count of three: one, two, three!"

Emily pressed down to take a photo, and she kept her finger in place so her camera would record photo after photo. She kept her eyes focused on the screen. For the first few seconds, she saw nothing unusual. Then, as the screen froze for a heartbeat to show the image the camera had just captured, she noticed a gray form near the front wall.

In each photo, the gray form became darker and less transparent. It was clearly a human shape. Emily's eyes flicked up from the screen, but when she looked directly at the spot, there was nothing there. Robert was only appearing in the photos. As each photo showed briefly on her phone screen, it gave Robert's movement an odd, stuttering effect, like a cartoon flip book whose pages were being riffled through a little too slowly.

Her eyes again fixed firmly on the screen, Emily saw the ghost moving closer. He reached the other side of the dining room table and just kept going, moving right through it and toward the photo of Eternal Rest. The second Robert's form made contact with his art, he gained speed so that he was suddenly rushing right at Emily. The entire screen was gray now. With a scream, Emily threw herself backward, pressing her body against the sideboard.

Emily's finger was still pressed on the camera button as the door flew open, and Reed and Trevor rushed in. "Emily?" Reed stopped and looked her over. "You're not hurt."

Ignoring him, Emily twisted around to look at the back wall. She tried taking photos of it, but there was no sign of Robert's ghost. Eventually, as the adrenaline began to disperse and her heartbeat slowed a little, she said, "That was intense, y'all."

Three loud knocks sounded from the wall where the sideboard sat. "Mrs. Thompson, are you okay?" Emily asked.

One knock sounded in answer: *yes*.

"Did the ghost give you a bit of a fright, too?"

Two knocks: *no*.

"Were you worried about me?"

Yes.

"That's sweet of you, Mrs. Thompson, but I'm fine. We think this ghost wants our help. He's not dangerous." *I hope.* For the first time, Emily wondered if Robert was singling her out—and trying to get her alone—not because he wanted her help, but because of some darker purpose. Emily couldn't imagine why Robert would have a vendetta against her, though, unless she was inadvertently responsible for his death. Her mind flashed back to the idea that someone had killed Robert because of his horribly altered photo of Eternal Rest, but that was an unlikely murder motive.

"Emily?" said a small voice from the doorway. Gretchen was glancing nervously behind her, toward the parlor. Her face had again lost all its color.

"Is my laptop acting up again?"

"No. I went to the desk to answer the phone, and the blank sheet of paper you have there suddenly had writing on it. I was alone in the room, and I swear I didn't do it. Do you think it's that ghost you told me about? The girl?" Gretchen raised her arm, and Emily could see she had the paper in her hand.

Kelly had written in such large letters that they covered the entire page: *Are you okay, Emily?*

"I'm fine, Kelly," Emily called out. She thought it was sweet her ghosts were so protective of her.

Soon, everyone was sitting down at the table, taking turns scrolling through the series of photos Emily had taken. There was no doubt Emily had captured Robert's ghost, but she still had no idea what he wanted to tell her. Still, it seemed like a good start.

Even though she was hesitant to be alone with Robert again, Emily knew it was necessary to get him to communicate further. She retrieved several sheets of printer paper from the desk and wrote the alphabet in large letters on them. Once they were laid neatly on the dining room table,

Emily reluctantly told everyone to head into the parlor to wait for her.

As soon as she was alone again, Emily readied her camera and said, "Robert, this time we're trying something different. I'm going to say 'now' every time I'm about to take a picture. I want you to spell out your message for me by pointing at a different letter in each photo. Do you understand?"

The photo of Eternal Rest didn't just tip over this time. It crashed down with such a loud bang that Reed actually knocked on the dining room door and asked Emily if she was all right.

"Okay, Robert. Here we go. Now!" Emily clicked once. "Now! Now! Now!"

Emily could see the gray arm that appeared in each of her photos, but she was so focused on keeping her camera steadily aimed at the letters that she didn't have a chance to see where the phantom hand was pointing. When the photos suddenly began to show nothing more than sheets of paper, Emily knew Robert must be finished with whatever he was trying to say.

Emily sat down at the table, pulling one of the sheets of paper toward her and flipping it over. She picked up her pen and poised it over the paper as she went back to the first photo in the series. Robert's ghost had fully understood her request, and a gray finger was clearly pointed at a letter in every shot. When she got to the end of the photos, Robert had spelled out an entire sentence, one that made Emily's breath catch in her throat: *She tricked me.*

24

Emily sat back, stunned. She stared at the words as questions flew through her mind. The biggest question, of course, was who the "she" Robert mentioned could be. Emily's thoughts immediately turned to Robert's wife, out there at the festival gleefully selling his art at exorbitant prices. Then, the image of Jess popped into Emily's mind, sitting there on the grass in front of the gazebo, crying.

Of course, Emily told herself, the mystery woman could be someone she didn't even know.

Putting the paper back into its proper spot, Emily stood and prepared to photograph the answer to another question. "Robert, who is the woman that tricked you?"

There was a sudden bang from upstairs. From the sound, Emily guessed it was another photo falling to the floor.

Reed, Trevor, and Gretchen were already rushing toward the stairs by the time Emily opened the door. She followed them upstairs, where they saw that not just one photo had been thrown from the wall, but all of the photos that lined the hallway.

"I don't understand," Emily said, partly to herself but also to Robert.

"What happened in there?" Trevor asked, already

bending down to pick up a photo. "Did he spell anything for you?"

Emily told the others about the cryptic message. "It makes some sense, I guess," she concluded. "He ingested a poisonous substance, which she probably slipped into his lunch. She tricked him into poisoning himself, and then she injected him with some more of it, just to be sure."

"What?" Gretchen's eyes were wide.

Oops. I probably wasn't supposed to share that detail. "I don't think the police are ready to announce that yet, but yes, the same stuff that he swallowed was also injected into his body a number of times."

Gretchen opened her mouth to respond, but the phone began to ring in the parlor. "I'll get it," she mumbled as she rushed downstairs.

Trevor and Reed helped Emily rehang the photos on the hallway walls. "I wonder why he chose to do this instead of spelling for me again?" Emily said. "I had just asked him what woman had tricked him when this happened."

"I hate to say it, but you do have three women staying with you this week," Reed said.

"Well, let's go downstairs and ask Robert if it's one of them." Emily glanced at Reed, whose mouth was set in a tight frown. She knew he hated even making the suggestion since he and Kat had been spending so much time together.

As the three of them reached the downstairs hallway, Emily could hear Gretchen's voice, artificially perky, saying, "Yes, Oak Hill is a great place for antiques shopping! It's just a short drive into downtown, so you can enjoy the peace and quiet at Eternal Rest while still being close to all the shops."

Reed and Trevor headed for the parlor as Emily went

into the dining room, shutting the door behind her. She pulled out her cell phone once again and aimed it at the alphabet, ready to snap pictures. "Robert," she called, "I have no idea why you threw all those photos to the floor, but you should know by now that we can't figure out what you're trying to say when you do that. I need you to be here, with me, so you can spell out more answers. Here's my first question for you: were you killed by your wife?"

Emily began taking photos while repeating, "Now!"

No gray arm appeared in any of the photos. Why was Robert being to stubbornly silent? Had she asked the wrong question?

"Let's try something different," Emily said. "Do you know who killed you? Now!"

Still, there was nothing. Emily lowered her phone and made an impatient noise. "Robert, I can't help you if you won't talk."

Emily gazed at the table, and suddenly she understood why Robert wasn't responding. The photo of Eternal Rest was gone.

Emily was in the parlor in seconds. "The artwork is missing." She looked directly at Gretchen as she spoke, since she had gone downstairs before the others. She was the only one who could have possibly taken it.

"The photo of Eternal Rest?" Trevor asked.

"Yes," Emily answered tersely. She didn't want to accuse Gretchen of the theft, but unless someone had snuck into the house and taken it, then there was no one else who could be responsible.

"Could one of the ghosts have taken it?" Reed asked. Emily could hear the doubt in his voice, and she saw his eyes dart toward Gretchen, as well.

"I suppose, but I don't know why they would." Emily sat down in one of the wingback chairs and massaged her temples. She needed to calm down and think before she said anything else. If she was going to accuse her assistant of stealing the photo, then that would imply Gretchen was involved in Robert's murder.

Maybe she loves true crime so much that she decided to do some of her own.

Emily took a few deep breaths. She knew everyone was watching her, waiting for her to speak, but she kept her eyes closed and her face tilted down. Could the "she" Robert mentioned mean Gretchen?

No, of course not. Gretchen has been here, working for me all week.

In fact, Emily realized, she had seen Gretchen at Eternal Rest, taking a reservation request, right before she drove into town to meet Trevor for coffee. Emily had been at the cemetery that morning, and she doubted Gretchen could have run into town, killed Robert, then returned, all in the short time Emily had been admiring Kat's art installation at Hilltop. Gretchen couldn't possibly have murdered Robert. Kat couldn't have done it, either, since she had been at the cemetery.

She tricked me.

The words played again and again in Emily's mind. Maybe the question wasn't who had tricked Robert, but why? It made the most sense that it was his wife. Emily had heard about artists' work shooting up in value posthumously, which meant Robert's wife surely knew about that phenomenon, too. If she wanted his money, then planning a murder right in the middle of the festival was a guaranteed way to make sure everyone knew about it. She could swoop in afterward, raise his prices, and get the money she felt she was owed.

While that certainly made the most sense, it still didn't explain why the altered photo of Eternal Rest had disappeared off the dining room table. Gretchen wouldn't have had any reason to take it, but then, the ghosts didn't have a reason, either. *Someone,* Emily told herself, *must have snuck in here while we were all upstairs.*

The security cameras could answer that question easily enough, but at the moment, it didn't seem as important as learning more about Robert's wife. In fact, as Emily had sat there, trying to sort through all the thoughts and suspicions fighting for attention in her mind, that feeling of urgency had begun to grow again. It was like something was tugging at her mind, demanding that she act quickly. Emily didn't know why, but for some reason, she felt an almost overwhelming urge to rush to the festival as quickly as possible.

Sage always tells me to trust my intuition.

"Right," Emily said, standing up straight and rolling her shoulders back decisively. "I'm going back to the festival."

"Why?" Reed asked.

"Because I think I know who killed Robert, and I want to ask her a few questions."

Reed stood and reached a hand toward Emily as if he might physically hold her back. "No, that's the job of the police."

"But—"

"*Emily.*"

Emily sighed. "You're right, Reed. I need to sit back and let Detective Hernandez handle this. But I'm still going back to the festival, because I just feel like I need to be there. I can't explain it."

Reed actually smiled. "I'm sure Sage could explain it."

"I'm going with you," Trevor said, rising.

"I'm going to stay here." Reed's voice was firm, and when he surreptitiously glanced at Gretchen again, Emily knew it was because he, too, was suspicious about the missing photo. He wanted to stay and keep an eye on her, Emily guessed, but what he said was, "After everything that has happened here today, I don't want Gretchen to be alone."

Gretchen smiled at Reed gratefully, but Emily saw how strained her expression was at the same time.

Soon, Emily was in her car, speeding toward Oak Hill with Trevor following right behind her. She called Danny on the way, telling him about Robert's message and her conclusion that he must have been talking about his wife.

"I'll be there in about ten minutes," Emily told him.

"I'll meet you at Robert's booth, but let me do the talking," Danny warned. "Remember, we can't accuse someone based on the word of a ghost, but I can chat with her about where she was when Robert was murdered. We hadn't asked her since we assumed she was nowhere near Oak Hill when it happened. That's my mistake."

"Trevor and I will just be little flies on the wall, pretending to look at art," Emily promised.

"And be careful," Danny added. "If your hunch is right, then she is not a woman you want to upset."

"Noted."

After Emily parked in the volunteer lot, she nearly ran to the square. Eventually, Trevor caught up to her and put a hand on her arm to slow her down. "Emily, it's okay. We're almost there."

Emily shook her head. "It's not okay. I've been getting these weird feelings all week, like something big is about to happen, or like there's something I have to do right now. I started feeling it at the house just now, in the parlor. It's like my brain is shouting at me to get to the festival as fast as possible, but I don't know why."

Trevor turned his head to give Emily a long look. "I think Reed was right. Sage would have an explanation for it. If you really are developing the ability to communicate with the dead, who knows what else you're learning to do?"

"I don't know that I like it."

"If it helps someone, even if that someone is a ghost trying to identify his killer, then isn't a little discomfort worth it?"

Emily stopped so she could turn her full attention to Trevor. "I suppose you have a good point," she said thoughtfully.

Trevor looked slightly embarrassed as he ducked his head. "I spent a lot of money in my early twenties, going to supposed psychics in an attempt to find out what happened to my brother. None of them told me anything that made me feel like their abilities were legitimate. After what I've experienced with you and Sage, though, I know there are people who really do have a connection to the other side, or whatever you call it. I wanted help and comfort back then, but I couldn't get it. Now, you have the chance to give help and comfort to someone else. That's a gift, Emily."

Emily gave a reluctant shrug. "You're right. I'll work on being grateful instead of completely weirded out. In the meantime, let's go find out why I'm so anxious to be at that booth."

Without waiting for Trevor, Emily turned and began walking quickly again. The two of them remained silent as they threaded through the crowd and made their way toward Robert's booth. As they got closer, Emily could see that only half a dozen altered photos were still hanging from the display racks. Clearly, Robert's widow had sold almost everything.

Even as Emily watched, the woman plucked a small piece off a nearby rack and handed it to someone standing in front of her. Emily realized with a start that it was Detective Hernandez.

As casually as possible, Emily slowed her pace and strolled up to the booth. Trevor stayed by her side, and together they edged closer to Danny while pretending to admire the art.

"Oh, are you actually ready to buy something this time?"

Emily's gaze shot to the woman, who was looking at her with one eyebrow raised and a judgmental little frown. Feeling called out and worried she was being too obvious, it took Emily a few tries before she finally answered, "I'm still on the fence."

The widow narrowed her eyes at Emily before turning her attention to Danny again. "As I was saying, this is one of his older pieces. I thought to bring some of Robert's earliest work with me."

Danny was nodding. "Good thinking. The artist was your husband, correct? What's your name?"

"Anita Gaines, though I doubt I'll keep that last name for long. I was going to change it the second our divorce was final."

"You're not worried that talking about how much you disliked him will raise suspicion?"

"I thought you were here to buy art, not to question me, Detective." Anita was now giving Danny the same look she had been giving Emily.

Danny smiled sweetly at Anita. "Sometimes it's hard to separate my work life from my personal life," he said smoothly. "I'm horrible on first dates, because apparently, I make it feel like an interrogation, but with wine."

Anita made a low sound that might have been a laugh. "You can suspect me all you want, Detective. I was at a day spa in Atlanta while Robert was here, dying on the ground in the middle of his stupid art. The staff at the spa will be happy to confirm that, I'm sure."

Emily bit her lip and forced herself to keep her eyes

fixed on the art in front of her. If Anita truly had an alibi, then who else would have had a reason to kill Robert?

As she stared at a piece of art hanging on the bottom of the rack, Emily suddenly understood why her feeling of urgency had been so strong.

"Danny," Emily said, reaching out a hand and waving toward him while keeping her eyes fixed on the photo.

As Danny closed the distance between himself and Emily, she could see Anita looking at them suspiciously out of the corner of her eye. Emily wasn't worried. She figured there was no point in Danny calling to check up on Anita's alibi, because Anita hadn't killed her husband.

To Emily's right, Trevor was bent at the waist, peering at the art as he tried to figure out what she was staring at so intently. "What am I missing?"

Instead of answering him, Emily spoke to Danny. "Tell me again about the substance that killed Robert," she said quietly, hoping Anita wouldn't overhear.

"Polyester resin," Danny said, sounding surprised.

"And what's it used for?"

"It's basically a plastic that you find in all kinds of places. My dad's fishing boat is coated in a layer of it to make it waterproof."

"Could you use it to make art?"

"Probably. People use all kinds of things to make art." Now Danny was also bent over as he looked closely at the altered photos hanging in front of them.

Emily stepped back and lowered her voice even more so no one could overhear her. Trevor and Danny pivoted to face her, the three of them standing in a tight knot. "Think about Jess, that girl who posed for Robert last year, only to see the photo of herself altered in such a disgusting way. Think about me, for that matter, and how upset I was to see Eternal Rest as the subject of one of Robert's pieces. Both of us had every right to be angry, but imagine how much more infuriating it would be if you were an artist, and another artist used an image of your work in their own. By photographing the sculpture in that bottom piece, Robert was trying to make money with someone else's art."

Danny brought his hand up in a cautioning gesture. "You're making an assumption, Emily. Maybe the sculptor gave him permission. It could even be a collaboration, and they were going to share the profit from the sale of this piece."

Emily shook her head vehemently. "No, they're not friends. She made that clear."

"She?"

"Marianne Callahan."

Trevor gasped. "The ghost said 'she' had tricked him."

Danny, however, looked at Emily shrewdly. "You think that's her sculpture in Robert's piece?"

Emily stepped forward again as Trevor and Danny made space for her to gaze at the altered photo. There was no doubt in her mind that the yellow angel—at least, that's what Emily assumed it was—with its spindly, outstretched arms and blank face, was Marianne's work. Robert had covered his photo of it with clippings from books. There were fat-cheeked cherubs smiling serenely across the top of the photo and little red devils waving pitchforks along the bottom. The wings of the sculpture were adorned with what appeared to be representations of the seven deadly sins. A scrawling, childish smiley face had been drawn onto the featureless head of the angel.

When Emily had picked up one of Marianne's sculptures, she had noticed how light it was. Looking at the pieces, one might assume they were carved from a colored stone or even painted. Instead, Emily guessed they were carved from polyester resin.

"There's only one sculptor at this festival whose work looks like that. We can prove it's one of her pieces right now," Emily said. "All we have to do is go over to her booth and ask her. Plus, you can examine her other work, and you'll see that it's made of a plastic sort of material."

"Anita," Danny said, turning quickly to Robert's widow, who was still staring at the three of them, even while several interested people tried to get her attention. Danny pointed at the photo with Marianne's angel sculpture in it. "We have to borrow this for a moment."

"The festival is about to close. I need to sell it!"

"I'm sorry. As of now, it's police evidence."

Anita looked at the photo like it had betrayed her, or as if Robert, even in death, had found one more way to keep her from the money she believed was rightfully hers. With a sneer, she said, "Fine." She snatched it off the rack and shoved it into Danny's hands.

Even as they were turning away to head to Marianne's booth, Emily overheard someone say to Anita, "Police evidence? Is it about the murder? I'll take the piece that was hanging right above it. I don't care what it costs!"

She's getting what she wants, and she didn't even have to kill him herself.

Danny was already on his phone as he, Emily, and Trevor were walking. As they turned down the row Marianne's booth was on, Roger Newton fell into step beside them. "You hang back, Miss Emily," he warned.

"I will," Emily answered in a sulking tone. Roger had a way of talking to her that made her feel a bit like a chastised child. He could be friendly and easy-going one minute, then launch into a lecture the next. Emily told herself he did it because he liked her and wanted to keep her from getting in over her head. Considering the messes she'd been in the midst of lately, she figured she needed someone like Roger in her life.

Marianne didn't seem to notice Emily was flanked by two people from the Oak Hill Police Department. Of course she didn't, Emily realized. Danny was dressed in black pants and a dark-gray polo shirt, and Roger blended into the crowd in his jeans and old concert T-shirt.

"Emily!" Marianne shouted, even though Emily had made it to within a few feet of her booth. Marianne pointed at a pale orange sculpture of a frog playing a violin. "That's my last one! I'm almost sold out! I've never had a weekend like this before!"

I'm sure you haven't.

Unsure how she should respond, Emily gave Marianne a tight smile that looked more like a grimace. She stopped walking, letting Danny and Roger move ahead of her. Trevor stood next to Emily, his feet spread apart and his shoulders tensed. After what he had been through with his father, Emily assumed Trevor took catching a murderer very seriously.

"Gentlemen," Marianne said, nodding at Danny and Roger. Her voice was as loud as ever. "I'll let you two fight over this last one, but whoever wins gets a discount since you're friends with Emily."

Emily swallowed. Her stomach suddenly seemed heavy, like a lead weight had settled there. She almost felt like she was betraying Marianne, coming here to accuse one of her own guests of murder. Emily didn't exactly like Marianne—her personality was a little too strong for Emily to feel much affection for the woman—but Marianne had never given Emily a reason to dislike her. And yet, here Emily was, possibly about to ruin Marianne's life.

She ruined her own life, Emily told herself firmly. *I'm helping Robert get justice, and that's the right thing to do.*

Emily didn't know if Trevor sensed her self-doubt, or if he was simply feeling as anxious as she was in that moment. Either way, he reached out and took her hand, giving it a strong squeeze.

"What's happening?" asked a quiet voice right between Emily and Trevor's heads.

Emily recoiled in surprise, clapping her free hand over her mouth to muffle a yelp. She whipped her head around to see Sage standing behind her and Trevor, her chin propped on Trevor's shoulder and her eyes wide as she watched Marianne.

"Sage, you nearly gave me a heart attack," Emily said quietly, her voice shaking.

"We've had enough death at this festival," Sage whispered loudly. "Is Marianne the one?"

"I believe so."

Emily and Sage fell silent so they could hear what Danny was now saying to Marianne. He must have introduced himself and Roger, because now Marianne had a slightly wary look on her face.

Danny had been holding Robert's artwork down by his side, and now he brought it up so that it was facing Marianne. "Is that your statue in this photo?"

"Sculpture," Marianne corrected defiantly. She looked from the photo to the orange frog, and Emily could see her jaw clenching. She seemed to realize the futility of a denial when the two pieces were so similar in style. "Yeah, that's one of mine. Why?"

Did you give Robert Gaines permission to use an image of your sculpture"—Danny emphasized the word, drawing it out pointedly—"in his artwork?"

"Of course not," Marianne scoffed. "That man had

zero respect for other artists. I'm not the only one whose work he stole."

"I'm not interested in other artists right now," Danny said firmly. "I'm interested in you. Were you angry about Robert Gaines using your art in his own?"

Now Marianne's head was pivoting between Danny and Roger, and she began to shrink back, as if she were afraid they might pounce on her at any moment. "No one likes having their art stolen." Emily had never heard Marianne's voice so quiet before. "Whenever Robert used someone else's art in one of his photos, the festival artists would all come together to complain, but he would always just give us that self-satisfied smile of his and tell us we were welcome to sue him. He knew no one ever would. It's just too expensive."

"Tell me, Marianne," Danny continued. "What are your sculptures carved from? They're not stone, obviously."

Marianne's lips drew together tightly. After a long pause, she said stiffly, "If you want to question me, Detective, you're welcome to do so at the police station. And I'd like to have a lawyer there."

"That can be arranged."

"Are you arresting me?"

"No. I simply want to have a chat." Danny sounded mildly threatening. "I'd like to ask that you remain here in Oak Hill until we've had a chance to speak. You're staying at Eternal Rest, right?"

Now Marianne's eyes fixed themselves on Emily's. "Yes," Marianne said, her voice louder again. Emily involuntarily took a step back, bumping into Sage. The resentment in Marianne's eyes and voice was frightening. If Emily had harbored any doubts before that this was a woman who was capable of murder, then they were gone now.

Marianne's chest heaved. "You stupid woman," Marianne said, still staring at Emily. "You and your stupid ghost chasing and séances." As she continued, her voice rose in volume until she was shouting. "Did you really think I would believe you were trying to get answers about your dead husband? I knew about all those photos of Robert's ghost. I knew that's who you were trying to contact with your little ghost-whisperer, there."

Sage made an angry noise as Marianne's eyes went to her.

Marianne began to shake her head violently. "None of it should have ever happened. You should have never been able to contact Robert's ghost. I tried to make sure of that, but that hateful man interrupted me."

"What man?" Emily asked, confused.

"Robert, of course," Marianne yelled. People walking nearby had stopped to watch the scene, her words carrying down the row. "You were about to drink the champagne when he made that loud noise, and you went running to investigate."

Now Emily felt even more confused. "I don't understand. What does our toast have to do with anything?"

"Because your glass was laced with the same stuff I used to kill Robert!" Marianne was screaming now.

Emily's mind flashed back to the horrible smell of the champagne. It hadn't smelled bad because it was cheap but because it had polyester resin mixed into it.

The ghost of Robert Gaines had saved her life.

Emily felt a wave of dizziness as she tried to process her thoughts. Vaguely, she felt Trevor's fingers squeeze hers harder and Sage's arm around her waist.

In front of her, Marianne Callahan began to run.

As soon as the last word was out of her mouth, Marianne spun on her heel and ran to the back of her booth. She deftly squeezed through a gap between the tent flaps and disappeared from sight.

"Split up!" Roger shouted at Danny. He was already pulling a radio from his hip, beginning to speak into it as he shot down the row to the right. Danny headed left, the crowd parting as gasps and even a few little screams could be heard.

Emily heard swearing behind her. "Wait 'til Jen and the rest of the festival staff hear about this," Sage said.

"Do you think they'll catch her?" Trevor asked.

"Where could she possibly go? They'll get her eventually." Sage sounded confident.

Emily was still standing there silently. Finally, Sage gave her a little nudge. "Hey, you okay?"

Am I? "No. One of my guests tried to kill me."

"But she didn't!" Sage said brightly. "Which is why we're going to open a bottle of wine tonight and toast to your living, breathing self."

One side of Emily's mouth turned up. "I'm not sure I ever want to take a drink again."

Sage waved dismissively. "Whatever. I'm not trying to kill you, so you have nothing to worry about."

Emily let go of Trevor's hand and wrapped her arms around herself, feeling a sudden chill. The sense of urgency had ebbed after she recognized Marianne's sculpture in Robert's photo. She had finally put the pieces together, so she had felt calmer. Now, though, the urgency returned, feeling like a sharp knock against her skull. Not knowing why she did it, Emily turned her head a little to the left as her arm shot out, a finger pointing toward the closed tent two down from Marianne's.

"Go, Trevor," Sage commanded.

Trevor lurched forward, and Emily knew Sage had given him a push. Not questioning the two women, he sprinted toward the spot Emily was indicating. He reached the front of the tent just in time to collide with Marianne, who came flying out from between the flaps. Trevor's arms closed around her as she struggled against him, trying to fend him off with her elbows and hands. Trevor kept his chin pointed up, and most of the blows failed to land against his face. Trevor's tall frame compared to Marianne's tiny one made it look like a parent was struggling with a child who was having a tantrum.

"What do we do?" Emily asked Sage, her words rolling together anxiously.

"We watch." Sage sounded completely calm, and soon Emily saw why. Two police officers were running down the row toward Trevor and Marianne. Trevor happily let go and stepped back, allowing the officers to put Marianne in handcuffs.

Soon, Marianne and the police were gone, and people in the row began slowly moving again. The air was buzzing with excited murmurs.

Emily realized she was clenching her fists, and she relaxed her hands, flexing her fingers while giving her arms a shake to loosen her taut muscles. "Did all of that really just happen?" she asked Sage incredulously.

"Yup."

"You're enjoying this way too much."

"The murderer has been caught, you somehow knew Marianne was going to run out of that closed tent, and you trusted your instincts enough to just go with it. She would have been caught eventually, but whatever flash of insight you got certainly speeded up the process. There is nothing strange about me enjoying this moment."

Emily turned to Sage, a small smile beginning to form on her lips. "And I'm still alive. You're right: we should be happy. And speaking of insight, I've been meaning to ask you about the Tarot cards. I pulled the Justice card one day, then the Seven of Swords. Later, the Five of Wands just showed up on the hallway floor. I got the first one before the murder, but I'm wondering if it's all related."

Sage narrowed her eyes thoughtfully. "Justice, deception, rivalry. You might have been subconsciously tapping into Marianne's feelings about Robert. She wanted justice, that's for sure. Well done, Em!"

"But how did the one card wind up in the hallway?"

Sage gave a short laugh. "I don't know! I think it's nice to have a little mystery in life."

"Maybe a little," Emily agreed grudgingly.

Trevor returned to them then, after chatting with several people who had stopped him, apparently wanting a firsthand account of his adventure.

"Congratulations on catching a killer," Emily said.

Instead of looking satisfied, Trevor simply looked thoughtful. "I just wish I could stop the murderers before they kill."

Emily knew Trevor was thinking not just about Marianne but about his dad, too. She squeezed his arm but remained silent, unsure what to say.

"Miss Emily," said a man's voice.

Emily turned to see Roger, his face flushed. He gave

Emily a bemused smile. "You always wind up in the middle of it, don't you? I'm sure glad that woman's attempt on your life failed."

"Me, too."

Roger looked at the three of them. "Y'all are becoming familiar faces at the station. Walk on over in the next hour or so, and we can take your statements."

Emily gave Roger a little salute. "See you soon."

Once Roger was gone, Sage said, "So Robert's ghost was trying to protect you Saturday night, when he threw your wedding photo across the room."

"Yeah. That was nice of him." Emily gazed thoughtfully at Marianne's orange frog sculpture. "And today, when I asked Robert who his mysterious 'she' was, I couldn't understand why he threw all the photos in the upstairs hallway instead of spelling out an answer. I bet he was trying to indicate it was Marianne, since her room was up there."

"He's not a very good communicator," Trevor noted.

"He wasn't a very good artist, either," Emily said. "Speaking of which, I wonder how Robert's photo of Eternal Rest figures into this? Did Marianne sneak into the house and steal it?"

"Maybe Robert moved it himself because he wanted you to stop talking to him and get to the festival in time to catch Marianne," Sage suggested.

"Maybe." Now that the excitement of Marianne's arrest was over, Emily realized how exhausted she was. She glanced at her watch, then at the few people still walking down the row. "The festival closes in five minutes."

"Thank goodness," Sage said.

"Trevor, would you like to join us at Eternal Rest tonight? We can figure out a dinner plan."

"I'm actually going to go home and take the longest, hottest shower of my life after I go give my statement. I just wrestled with a killer, and I want to wash every trace of her off my body." Trevor kept his tone light, but his expression showed how serious he was. "After that, I'm going to sleep, no matter what time it is."

"Thanks for everything, Trevor. Next week, assuming no one else gets murdered, let's actually get that coffee."

Trevor winked at Emily. "Sounds like a plan." He ruffled Sage's spiked hair before walking away.

"As for me," Sage spoke up, "I'm going to go pack up my booth. I'm definitely stopping by later, though. Jen will be here late, so if you're offering to make dinner, I wouldn't say no."

Emily laughed. Life had been strange lately, but at least her best friend was still as predictable as ever.

When Emily walked in the front door of Eternal Rest, she could hear Gretchen in the parlor, saying little except for outbursts of surprise. Emily knew Gretchen was on the phone, listening to the gossip from the arts festival, when she said excitedly, "She's staying here! I met her!"

Emily walked into the parlor and sank into one of the wingback chairs, choosing to ignore Gretchen for the moment. She had offered to stay and help Sage pack up, and the work went quickly with two of them tackling it. They had then walked to the police station together to share what they had witnessed at the festival that day. Emily refrained from mentioning Robert's ghost when she gave her statement, saying only that she had made the connection to Marianne when she had spotted the yellow angel in one of Robert's photos.

Gretchen abruptly said, "Oh, hey, I gotta go." She put her phone away and glanced toward Emily, embarrassed. "Sorry. That was a friend of mine. She was filling me in."

Emily sat up straight. "Where's Reed?"

"He went to the festival to help Kat pack up her booth. I guess once the police learned it was Marianne and arrested her, he figured I wasn't in any danger here."

Gretchen cleared her throat and shifted from one foot to the other, her eyes staring at the floor. She grasped at her hair, and one finger twisted nervously around a curl. "Um, Emily, I need to tell you something."

"I'm listening."

"I stole that photograph of Eternal Rest." Gretchen's voice sank so low that Emily could barely hear her.

Even though Emily had suspected Gretchen of taking the photo, she still felt shocked to hear her actually confessing it. More curious than angry, Emily prompted, "Why?"

Gretchen swallowed hard. "Earlier in the week, I stopped by the pharmacy before I came here for work. I had to get my father-in-law's prescription." Gretchen stopped and looked at Emily expectantly.

"I remember."

"Well, when I got home that night, I couldn't find the bag. I looked everywhere for it, and I thought maybe I had forgotten it here. So, the next morning, I looked here, but I still couldn't find it."

Emily frowned. "What does this have to do with you stealing the photo?"

Gretchen's face tightened, and Emily could see tears shining in her eyes. "Because," she said quickly, "I thought I had just lost the bag, which wasn't a big deal. But then, today, you said Robert was injected with the stuff that killed him. All I could think about was how my father-in-law's insulin syringe had gone missing, and I was afraid that was what the murderer had used. I panicked, because I thought I might be an accomplice to murder, and so I hid the photo so that Robert's ghost couldn't talk to you anymore."

Gretchen covered her face with her hands, her shoulders shaking as she cried softly.

Stunned, Emily simply sat there for a moment. "It's very likely Marianne did use the syringe. She could have easily taken it from the desk." Emily tried to speak gently but loud enough to be heard over the sound of Gretchen's crying. "That doesn't mean you're an accomplice, though. You've done nothing wrong."

Gretchen took a deep, stuttering breath and rubbed her face on her sleeve. "I know. I realized that after you left to go back to the festival. In the moment, though, I just panicked. I'm so sorry."

A relieved little laugh escaped Emily's mouth. "I actually suspected you of taking it, but that made me also suspect you might have killed Robert. I had to think back to the day he was killed, and I realized you were here at the house, so you couldn't have done it. Gretchen, you need to stop by the police station on your way home. Ask for Danny Hernandez. He'll be very interested in what you have to say about the syringe."

"Okay. Oh, and here's the photo." Gretchen reached behind the desk and pulled it out. The frame had been just narrow enough to fit between the desk and the wall.

"I don't want it," Emily said honestly. "Why don't you keep it? A little souvenir of your adventure in true crime."

"Really? Thank you!"

She has terrible taste in art, but she's a good assistant.

"Gretchen, I know it's been a rough week, but you're really good at this job. If you promise not to hide any of my things anymore, I'd like you to work here permanently."

Gretchen bit her lip and looked down at the photo. "That's nice of you," she said slowly, "but it turns out I prefer getting my true crime fix on TV, not in real life. It's a little too exciting here."

"It's not normally like this." *Except for lately*, Emily added silently.

Apparently, Gretchen was having the same thought. "One of your guests was murdered a few weeks ago. No, I need a quieter job."

"Understood," Emily said. "Thank you for the great work this week, though. I hope to run into you around town. Maybe I'll get to meet your son sometime."

"I'd like that. Thank you, Emily. I'll head to the police station now, like you suggested."

As Gretchen closed the front door behind her, Emily felt a wave of disappointment. *How many assistants am I going to go through?*

Emily's stomach growled in answer, and she realized she was starving after such an intense day. Just as Emily got to work making dinner, she heard the front door open, followed by a lot of footsteps in the hallway. Soon, Sage appeared in the kitchen doorway. "We're all eating here tonight, but you're not cooking. We have takeout from The Depot."

Kat appeared behind Sage. "And I'm opening up that bottle of wine I brought to share with you!"

"You know," Emily said in a mockingly serious tone. "Our work isn't done yet."

"I know," Sage said happily. "We still have to get Robert to cross over."

27

As Emily put the things she had pulled out of her refrigerator back into it, she heard even more footsteps in the hallway and knew it wasn't just her guests in the house. When she walked into the parlor, she saw Jake, Selena, and Kat, as well as Reed, Sage, and her mom. Smiling, Emily said, "What is this, another celebration?"

Jake groaned. "Not like the one we had last night. And I wouldn't call it a celebration. More of a…"

"It is a celebration," Selena said firmly. "It's been a hell of a festival in more ways than one, but more than anything, we're celebrating the fact that you're alive and well, Emily. We heard about Marianne's confession." Selena gave a little shudder.

"Oh! Speaking of which, I'm going to get some wine glasses out of the kitchen." Kat popped up from her seat on the couch and winked at Emily. "Don't worry, I'll let you pour your own wine."

Kat was soon back with a laden tray, and in a few minutes, everyone was raising a glass as she prepared to give a toast. Every hand froze in mid-air at the sound of the front door. There were slow, heavy footsteps, and then a massive form appeared in the doorway.

"Am I too late?" Greg asked quietly.

"Not at all," Emily assured him. She looked over and

realized Kat had already poured an extra glass of wine, and Emily picked it up and handed it to Greg.

"That woman was not nice," Greg said.

Kat laughed. "That is the perfect toast for this occasion! That woman was not nice, and we're all happy to be here, together and safe."

Everyone raised their glasses again.

"Now," Sage said, after taking a long drink. "It's time to send Robert on to his next artist-in-residence adventure. Em, get out that photo of Eternal Rest so we can communicate with him."

"Oh, uh, I don't have it. I gave it to my assistant."

"Emily!" Rayna had a shocked expression on her face.

"Sorry, Mom, but after this week, I don't want to see that photo ever again."

Rayna looked disappointed, but she shrugged good-naturedly. "I get it."

"How are we supposed to communicate with Robert, then?" Reed asked. "It seemed like his ghost was pretty firmly tied to his own art."

Everyone looked at each other for a moment, trying to think of an alternative solution. "I know!" Emily finally said. "We can find some of his work online, and use that. He haunted my laptop once before." She walked over to her desk, and as she put her wine glass down, she realized the paper she kept there for Kelly to write on had a message on it. At first, Emily assumed Gretchen had jotted down some notes, probably while on the phone, but then she recognized Kelly's big, swooping letters.

Emily gasped. "Kelly says he already left. I wonder if he crossed over, or if I accidentally sent Gretchen home with a ghost?"

Everyone just laughed in response, and Emily eventually joined in, telling herself that Robert's ghost was harmless, and if he was still haunting the photo of Eternal Rest, then it wouldn't really be a problem. Even if it was, Gretchen could just call on Emily and Sage to come have a chat with him.

As Selena launched into a story about a customer who wanted to order fifty painted clay pots as Christmas presents for their employees, Jake slipped out of the room. When he returned, he was carrying a large white frame. Whatever was in the frame was facing Jake, so no one could see it.

Selena broke off when she saw what Jake had in his hands, and he began, "Emily, none of us liked the way Robert depicted Eternal Rest, and we know it was even more upsetting for you. Robert said he was showing your B and B in its real form, but of course that's not true. He created an Eternal Rest that doesn't exist, so I wanted to show it for what it really is: warm, welcoming, and bright."

Jake turned the frame around, and Emily found herself looking at an exquisite oil painting of her home. The house looked cozy nestled between oaks and pines, and a golden light was pouring out of the front windows. The dogwoods that flanked the porch stairs were in full bloom. Above, instead of the dark, nightmare sky Robert had depicted, the crisp blue sky had just a few wispy clouds floating across it.

"Oh!" Emily said. It was all she could get out in her surprise and gratitude. She blinked a few times and sniffed loudly, which made Sage chuckle. Emily threw Sage a look, but at least the distraction kept her from crying right there in front of everyone. "Jake, it's just perfect. Thank you. When did you have time to paint this?"

"I do live painting every day at the festival. You saw the cabin I had in progress. I knew you might come by before your shift each day, so that's when I painted the cabin. In the afternoons, when you were busy volunteering, I painted

Eternal Rest. I'm just happy no one saw it and told you. I would have hated to ruin the surprise."

"I'll be proud to hang it here. Thank you, again."

"And thank you, Emily," Kat spoke up. "You and Eternal Rest help make this one of our favorite festivals on the circuit, and we look forward to staying here with you again next year. Just get a full background check on whoever gets to stay in Marianne's old room, okay?"

Everyone laughed and raised their glasses to toast to that.

A NOTE FROM THE AUTHOR

Thank you for reading *Picture Perfect!* I really appreciate the support I get from readers like you, because it allows me to continue telling stories. I can't wait for you to read what's next for Emily! In the meantime, will you please leave a review for this book? It means so much to indie authors like me.

Thank you,

Beth

ACKNOWLEDGMENTS

As always, I am in debt to my fabulous test readers Brenda, David, Kristine, Lisa, Mom, and Sabrina. They are kind but honest in their feedback, and I'm a better storyteller because of them. My editors Lia and Nicole and my marketing/design pro Jena at BookMojo ensure my work is polished and presentable.

NEXT IN THE SERIES

**Find out what's next for Emily, Sage,
and the ghosts of
Eternal Rest Bed and Breakfast!**

Scenic Views
ETERNAL REST BED AND BREAKFAST BOOK FOUR
PARANORMAL COZY MYSTERIES

Guests are seeing the dead at Eternal Rest Bed and Breakfast.

Eternal Rest Bed and Breakfast seems quiet after Emily Buchanan sends the resident ghosts on a mission to find her late husband's spirit. When she begins hearing strange noises, Emily doesn't think it can be paranormal. After all, there are no ghosts left in the Victorian mansion. Right?

Emily realizes she bought more than a mirror when she finds herself face-to-face with a ghost trapped inside it. The ghost's story leads Emily to an historic mansion that has been wreathed in mystery for years.

As the suspects add up, so do the number of threats Emily and her friends are receiving. Someone among the living desperately wants them to give up the search for clues. Emily worries even more about her safety when she finds out something evil is lurking just outside the town of Oak Hill…

BOOKS BY BETH DOLGNER

The Eternal Rest Bed and Breakfast Series
Paranormal Cozy Mystery
Sweet Dreams
Late Checkout
Picture Perfect
Scenic Views
Breakfast Included
Groups Welcome
Quiet Nights

The Betty Boo, Ghost Hunter Series
Paranormal Romance
Ghost of a Threat
Ghost of a Whisper
Ghost of a Memory
Ghost of a Hope

The Nightmare, Arizona Series
Paranormal Cozy Mystery
Homicide at the Haunted House
Drowning at the Diner
Slaying at the Saloon
Murder at the Motel
Poisoning at the Party
Clawing at the Corral

Manifest
Young Adult Steampunk
A Talent for Death
Young Adult Urban Fantasy

Non-Fiction

Georgia Spirits and Specters
Everyday Voodoo

ABOUT THE AUTHOR

Beth Dolgner writes paranormal fiction and nonfiction. Her interest in things that go bump in the night really took off on a trip to Savannah, Georgia, so it's fitting that her first series—Betty Boo, Ghost Hunter—takes place in that spooky city. Beth also writes paranormal nonfiction, including her first book, *Georgia Spirits and Specters*, which is a collection of Georgia ghost stories.

Beth and her husband, Ed, live in Tucson, Arizona. Their Victorian bungalow is possibly haunted, but it's not nearly as exciting as the ghostly activity at Eternal Rest Bed and Breakfast.

Beth also enjoys giving presentations on Victorian death and mourning traditions as well as Victorian Spiritualism. She has been a volunteer at an historic cemetery, a ghost tour guide, and a paranormal investigator. Beth likes to think of it all as research for her books.

Keep up with Beth and sign up for her newsletter at
BethDolgner.com.

Manufactured by Amazon.ca
Bolton, ON

43668385R00118